PRAISE FOR LAST LIGHT

"In Kansas at the height of WWII, Farnsworth presents a U.S. Army Hospital where injured and ill American soldiers and German prisoners of war exhibit all the traits and complications of a complex and intimate world. Here a young interpreter begins to unravel one prisoner's secrets, which leads to a crime she must overcome in order to survive."

—Linda Spalding
Author of The Follow *and recipient of the 2012 Canadian Governor-General's Literary Award for her novel,* The Purchase

---

"This extraordinary short novel, compact and complex, beautifully evokes the innocence of a Kansas childhood, a woman's sexual and intellectual awakening, and the physical and psychic wounds of war with its inherent moral ambiguities. The central question—When is killing justified?—haunts until the end."

—Marion Abbott
Former co-owner of Mrs. Dalloway's Bookstore, Berkeley, California

"In 1943, a young woman is hired to interpret for German prisoners of war at a U.S. Army Hospital in Kansas. Harboring dark secrets from her childhood, Isabelle Graham will be forced into a struggle that saves her own life as well as others in the distant, on-going war. Farnsworth has written in *Last Light* a thrilling and moving account of a young woman's courage and determination in the face of seemingly insuperable odds."

—John Balaban
Passing Through a Gate, *A collection of John Balaban's poems, essays, and translations, will be published spring 2024 by Copper Canyon Press. Twice a National Book Awards poetry finalist, he is the author of* Remembering Heaven's Face: A Story of Rescue in Wartime Vietnam

---

"With delicacy and grace, Farnsworth illuminates a moment in history all but lost to memory. The remarkable novel manages to be compelling as a war story, a love story, and even a western! What a gift it was to read."

—Ayelet Waldman
Author of the novel Love and Treasure
and Executive Producer of Netflix's Unbelievable

"Farnsworth demonstrates mastery of complexity: What's the collateral damage of war on those behind the lines who never see combat themselves but must handle the fallout? And how should we respond to the epiphany that nobody, even a fictional character, comes through real conditions with entirely clean hands? Farnsworth has dreamed up a revelation with power and insight on every page."

—Douglas Foster
Author of After Mandela: The Struggle for Freedom in Post-Apartheid South Africa; *Contributor to* The Atlantic *and* The American Scholar, *among other publications; Professor, Medill School of Journalism, Northwestern University*

Additional endorsement on the back cover from:

Michael D. Mosettig, *Foreign Affairs and Defense Senior Producer and Editor of* The PBS NewsHour *from 1985 to 2012, who has written for, among other publications,* The Economist, The New Republic, *and the* Online NewsHour

LAST
LIGHT

Elizabeth Farnsworth

Elizabeth
Farnsworth

Flint Hills Publishing

Cover photo part of a larger image by Terry Evans
www.terryevansphotography.com

German translations by Karina Epperlein

Cover Design by Amy Albright
stonypointgraphics.weebly.com

Flint Hills Publishing

Topeka, Kansas
Tucson, Arizona
www.flinthillspublishing.com

Printed in the U.S.A.

Paperback Book: ISBN: 978-1-953583-81-9
Hardback Book ISBN: 978-1-953583-84-0
Electronic Book ISBN: 978-1-953583-82-6

Library of Congress Control Number: 2024903131

*"Every fairy tale had a bloody lining.
Every one had teeth and claws."*

Alice Hoffman, *The Ice Queen*

.

This story, though fiction, was inspired by actual events, people, and even a horse, Flag, who was much loved by my sister, Marcia. She died in Salina, Kansas, in 2022. This book is dedicated to her.

Marcia Fink Anderson
1937-2022

Prologue

FEBRUARY 1934

A girl and a young man sit side by side in a Viennese café, leafing through tales by the Brothers Grimm. Isabelle Graham is 13, old enough to resent the dark-haired beauty across the room making eyes at her tutor, Otto Maurer, who savors an espresso as he prepares to teach his favorite fairy tale to a student he enjoys.

"I found it," he shouts, drawing more stares from around the room. "They saved 'The Juniper Tree' for last!"

A studious, politically engaged young man, Otto has wavy black hair and eyes the color of his espresso. He'd be surprised to learn that Isabelle is determined to marry him under stained glass windows in the nearby Votivkirche when she turns 18 and he is 28. Her family attends Sunday services at the church, delighting as the colors around them blaze in the light of the rising sun.

Now, between sips of heiße Schokolade mit Schlagobers (hot chocolate with whipped cream), Isabelle smooths her Scotch plaid skirt and brushes back a lock of hair that has escaped her ponytail. Otto is about to read short passages from "The Juniper Tree," which Isabelle will try to translate into English. He has given her a list of words to memorize: geschlachtet (butchered), seidenes Tuch (silken cloth), Mühlstein (millstone). Impressed by her progress since arriving in Vienna the previous September, Otto has told friends that his pupil has a rare instinct for German. He has taught her in museums, palaces, and theaters, but she most

enjoys translating tales of woe and wonder over hot choco-
late in the Café Landtmann. Otto reads:

> *Das ist nun lange her, wohl an die zweitausend*
> *Jahre, da war einmal ein reicher Mann, der hatte*
> *eine schöne fromme Frau, und sie hatten sich beide*
> *sehr lieb, hatten aber keine Kinder.*

Isabelle translates:

> *It's now a long time ago, about two thousand*
> *years perhaps, that there was a rich man who had*
> *a beautiful, good-hearted wife, and they loved each*
> *other very much, but had no children.*

"*Gut gemacht,*" *Otto says.* "*Well done. I like your use*
of 'perhaps' in the first sentence: 'A long time ago, about
2,000 years 'perhaps'... What does that sentence tell you?"

Isabelle starts to say she doesn't understand the ques-
tion when a man at a nearby booth coughs and clears his
throat in an obvious attempt to get their attention. Rising
from his seat, he asks permission to interrupt the lesson. Otto
nods his assent and stands to greet the stranger, who looks
to be in his fifties. He's tall with a well-trimmed mustache
and black, thinning hair. He wears a light brown suit of very
fine wool. Approaching their table, he bows formally.

"*Mein Herr, I hope we haven't annoyed you?*" *Otto*
asks in German.

"*Not at all,*" *the intruder responds.* "*'The Juniper Tree'*
is a favorite of mine and I salute you for teaching it. May I
ask a question?"

*"Please do," Otto replies.
"What does that first sentence tell **you**?"
"It signals timelessness."*
The stranger nods vigorously. *"Those words transport
us to the deepest part of ourselves. Of course, the story is
fearsome—furchterregend. A boy is born to the first wife,
who dies when the child is still very young. The father re-
marries and a daughter, Marlinchen, is born. That wife is
wicked. She murders the boy, hacks him to pieces and stews
them in a sour broth, which she feeds to his father. The theme
appears elsewhere in literature—think of Thyestes—but the
dreadful beauty of 'The Juniper Tree'—the transformation
of the murdered boy into a vengeful bird—is unique in my
view."*

Isabelle doesn't understand every word but likes
"dreadful beauty" as a description of the tale. The stranger
returns to his own booth and continues to eavesdrop, nod-
ding vigorously when she interprets well and sighing audibly
when she doesn't.

Otto reads the final sentence, and Isabelle translates:

*"There were steam and flames and fire rising
from the place, and when that was over, the little
brother stood there, and he took his father and
Marlinchen by the hand, and the three of them were
so happy and went into the house and sat down at
the table and ate together."*

The intruder stands again and exclaims loudly enough
for everyone in the café to hear, *"It's hervorragend—mag-
nificent—a fractured world made whole again."* Then he

dons his heavy coat and returns to Otto's and Isabelle's table, bowing as he says goodbye. Otto stands and nods, his way of showing respect. At the front door of the café, the stranger turns for a final look before disappearing down the street. Otto collapses in his seat. Something momentous has occurred and Isabelle waits for an explanation.

"That was Stefan Zweig," Otto whispers, "in my opinion, the world's greatest living author. He is a Jew and lives in Salzburg, where fascism is ascendant. I fear he's on his way into exile."

EARLY AUGUST 1943

Isabelle stays in the shadows to avoid notice and wonders why the hospital train bypassed the Santa Fe Station in East Topeka and stopped at a railroad crossing south of town. On the train are ill and wounded German prisoners of war. Perhaps the Army thought they'd meet protests or worse at the downtown station? The only light comes from inside the train and from lanterns carried by military police. It should be easy for Isabelle to avoid notice. The Army has declared the train off-limits to reporters, but her editor, disobeying the order, has sent her, the newspaper's only German-speaking reporter, to cover the first POWs to arrive for treatment at the new U.S. Army general hospital west of town.

When four ambulances arrive, soldiers from the hospital detachment grab litters and board Pullman cars. The transfer of the most seriously wounded or ill men is efficient. Within 15 minutes, the ambulances leave—no sirens—and head west on 21ˢᵗ Street. Four city buses take their place. Ambulatory patients line up inside the cars of the train. Through windows, Isabelle sees bandaged faces, arms in slings. MPs and orderlies rush to help injured men down the steps. Steam and smoke billow from the huge engine. The scene is hellish, something out of Goya or Doré, Isabelle thinks. The patients make their way in lantern-light to buses. Neighbors in robes and pajamas have come out of houses to watch from front porches. Someone shouts, "They're Germans!" Several rocks are thrown but no one is hit.

MPs run to protect the prisoners, and drivers hurry to load their buses. Isabelle slips into a line of men waiting to board. One asks loudly in German, "Where are we?"

"Kansas," Isabelle says.

"Wo zum Teufel ist Kansas? Where in the hell is Kansas?"

"In the center of the United States."

"A long way from the ocean?"

"Yes."

"Verdammt! Harder to escape."

The line is moving quickly. She'll be ordered to leave any minute. She asks the man in front of her, "Where did you come from?"

"Tunisia via Casablanca and a hospital on Staten Island," he says in German.

"Where's your home?"

"Regensburg," he answers proudly. Other prisoners also shout the names of their towns:

Aachen, Lübeck, Heidelberg, Linz.

Isabelle notes that at least one prisoner is Austrian.

Before slipping away, she asks another man, "What is your illness or injury?"

"Hepatitis. Your people weren't prepared for the tens of thousands of us taken prisoner in Tunisia. The filth in those camps sickened and sometimes killed us."

Hearing the conversation, an MP yells at Isabelle to "Beat it!" In the darkness, she runs to the newspaper's car, drives downtown to the office, and dictates her story to the night editor, who cuts out the reference to Goya and Doré. It's late, and Isabelle is tired, but before going home, she gets permission to spend the next day at the new hospital reporting on the POWs.

"I'll ride Joe," she tells her editor. "No German male can resist a good-looking horse."

Chapter 1

JULY – AUGUST 1933

During the summer before their year in Vienna, Isabelle Graham spent almost every day with her cousin Diane, who was a year older and lived on the western edge of Topeka with her parents and two younger brothers. In their large backyard were homing pigeons, chickens, two goats, and a German short-haired pointer named Roy. Isabelle loved the menagerie and worshipped Diane, who, like Isabelle, was tall for her age with long legs and light brown hair held back on both sides by barrettes. People often asked if the girls were twins, or at least sisters, which thrilled Isabelle, an only child.

That summer, Diane was obsessed with light and the vision of certain creatures, including bees—what and how they *see*. She brought books home from the Topeka library and explained to Isabelle that, unlike humans, bees can see ultraviolet light. Sunflowers and pansies, for example, have nectar guides that can only be seen in that spectrum, Diane said.

When Isabelle spent the night, which was often, the girls got up before dawn and followed a path leading west from Diane's house to a place high enough on the prairie to see first light, which they considered almost holy.

West of Topeka, the Kansas landscape rises gradually to the Flint Hills, which stretch from Nebraska south to Oklahoma. Because of close-to-the-surface chert and limestone (the remains of shellfish from an ancient sea), the hills remained mostly unplowed. The girls believed that birds sing at dawn to celebrate the miracle of light, which shouldn't be taken for granted. Sometimes the rising sun encircled the State Capitol like a halo. Other mornings, haze diffused the rays, and the sky became a kaleidoscope of colors—purple, pink, orange—always new combinations.

In a ravine by a creek in those hills, Isabelle and Diane built a hideout—they called it Wildland—with twigs and branches from mulberry bushes and cottonwood trees to provide shelter from storms. They gathered and dried coneflower, goldenrod, and black-eyed Susan, pressing petals at home between pages of *The Encyclopedia Britannica*. They collected evidence of coyote kills: the femur of a fawn, skulls of mice and raccoons. On the few cool days of that very hot summer they built a fire to heat Campbell's Soup, mixing it with water from the creek. Some days they lay for hours among wildflowers and tall grasses, watching clouds billow overhead.

One day an eagle swooped down and lifted a baby rabbit to its death. Roy, Diane's dog, lunged, but too late. Hawks occasionally snatched fledglings from nests along the creek. At first, the girls tried to save small creatures from predators, but eventually they accepted that nature's way was to eat or be eaten.

The grasses also hid nests of grasshoppers, sparrows, and meadowlarks. Isabelle and Diane heard grasshoppers sing by rubbing the surface of their legs against a wing. In the evening, cicadas sang as loud as any creature, including Isabelle and Diane.

Visiting Isabelle's Presbyterian Sunday school one day, Diane asked the minister if the prairie surrounding Topeka was an *emanation* of God. She often looked up words in the dictionary before asking grownups difficult questions.

"The prairie inspires awe," she said. "At times it's so bright we can't see, and its darkness blinds us at night. We find it holy. Do you?"

The minister paused to think and then explained that the word "holy" had originally meant "whole," "complete." He agreed that prairie contained that attribute but not in the same way as God. At home later, Diane vigorously disagreed.

"Don't believe everything he says, Isabelle. We must decide for ourselves."

Unlike her cousin, Isabelle believed that the minister had an inside track to truth. She and Diane were just children, after all. Isabelle attended Sunday school and sang in the youth choir in their church, where her parents were lay leaders. Diane had come into the world a skeptic. Nature and science were her religion.

At the end of June that summer, the girls' parents bought each of them a horse—a buckskin named Penny for Diane and a sorrel for Isabelle named Joe. Around Topeka, even people without much money sometimes kept a horse in their yard or at a farm near town. Penny and Joe were three-year-old Quarter Horses trained to herd cattle. The girls' fathers trailered the horses from a ranch to a small pig farm about a mile southeast of Diane's house. A man named Daniel Jones owned the farm.

Now began a series of further adventures which included the farmer. The girls first called him Mr. Jones and then Danieljones, running his two names together. A tall, skinny man who seemed old to Isabelle and Diane, he was

25. The pigs he kept penned up near the barn didn't demand much time, and the girls soon guessed that he was lonely and enjoyed their company. At first, he watched as they lured their horses from the pasture with sugar cubes and led them back to the barn, standing on stools for the heavy saddling, but before long, Danieljones was helping. When he noticed they weren't venturing far beyond the path alongside the creek on his farm, he saddled Amber, his roan mare, and guided Isabelle and Diane to nearby berry patches, and when they begged to go further, to natural springs in the Flint Hills. Sometimes a snake or field mouse would startle the horses, and Danieljones taught the girls how to keep from falling.

"You press your knees into the saddle, like this," he said, demonstrating how to stay on a horse that had reared up. "Hold tight around the neck if you can reach or grab the mane. Keep your head down in case your horse throws back his head. You don't want to get hit by that head."

The girls learned that their new friend had made some money and gained local fame busting broncos before the Depression closed most rodeos in Kansas. He'd used his small savings to buy the pig farm. Diane and Isabelle treated him with respect because he was older, and he treated them like his younger sisters back home on a farm three hours west of Topeka. "You remind me of them," he said.

During that summer, he taught the cousins the skills they would need for competing in horse shows. They learned to rope, cut cattle (practicing on his pigs), and barrel race. In late August, their parents offered to pay Danieljones to keep training the girls during the winter, and he agreed. He said he'd have done it for fun but was grateful for the money.

Diane and Isabelle hoped to stay in shape for summer competitions by riding throughout the winter.

But in September, two weeks after school started, Isabelle's father received a coveted fellowship to study advanced surgery at the Medical University of Vienna. They would leave home immediately. Isabelle convinced her father not to sell Joe, but to let him stay with Diane's horse at the pig farm.

The Grahams took two different trains to New York, a passenger ship to France, and then another train to Vienna, where they lived for a year, returning to Topeka before school started in the fall of 1934.

On their second day home, Isabelle's parents drove her to the farm and followed her as she walked to the pasture gate. When Joe came running, Isabelle laughed with pleasure, pleasing her mother and father. She knew they hoped riding her horse would ease her melancholy, which had begun when Isabelle's Viennese tutor, Otto Maurer, mysteriously disappeared. For half a year, Isabelle had spent five days a week with Otto, and then suddenly, under confusing circumstances, he was gone. Besides studying German, they had ridden horses together in the Prater and attended productions of the State Opera, where standing in back was cheap. The loss of Otto had left Isabelle "unmoored," a word her parents used. Back in Kansas with her cousin, Isabelle helped rebuild Wildland and gathered more flowers and bones, but one afternoon as they lay side-by-side under the autumn sun, Diane said, "You've gone dark. What snuffed out your light?"

After a long pause, Isabelle answered, "I'm just tired after the long trip home."

It was the only lie she ever told her cousin.

AUGUST 1943

Despite her late-night assignment at the hospital train, Isabelle woke up early the next morning and joined her parents for breakfast at the dining room table, where they also gathered for meals, board games, and sometimes just to converse. A 1,000-piece puzzle of the pyramids at Giza covered one corner of the table. Anne, Isabelle's mother, served scrambled eggs and fresh berries from her victory garden. In spite of rationing, the Grahams ate well from their garden and from produce provided by friends who lived on farms. Anne left her seat occasionally to replenish seeds on a bird feeder at a large, south-facing window. Nearly a dozen red-winged blackbirds feasted there.

After finishing his breakfast, Isabelle's father, William, picked up the *Topeka Daily Capital* and read the front-page headline aloud: "Catania Falls to British. Axis Bastion on East Coast of Sicily which has Withstood Siege Since July 15 Finally Cracks Before Smashing Assault of the Eighth Army.

"The article goes on to describe signs of an imminent

Nazi withdrawal from Sicily," William added. "It's the best news since victory in Tunisia."

The Grahams' dining room opened on the west into a spacious living room and, on the east, a sunroom. Windows were open, and a warm wind blew through the brown shingle bungalow, which sat on a large corner lot in a century-old, affluent neighborhood of cobblestone streets and mostly large, Victorian houses. Neighbors who'd considered the Arts and Crafts design of the Graham house too small and plain for their street had tried, but failed, to block its construction. Isabelle had once heard two neighbors whispering among themselves that the Grahams, while nice, were "different." From their tone of voice, Isabelle understood the comment as criticism. Anne's abolitionist grandparents had left a prosperous Connecticut farm in 1855 to come to Kansas by riverboat and covered wagon with a trunkful of "Beecher's Bibles," the Sharps rifles favored by anti-slavery activists willing to shed blood for the cause. John Brown had arrived in the state the same year, and after pro-slavery forces sacked Lawrence, Brown and a band of followers, including four of his sons, slaughtered five pro-slavery men living along Pottawatomie Creek, 70 miles southeast of Topeka. Family lore maintained that Anne's grandfather rode with John Brown, though perhaps not on that night.

"Do you think your grandfather killed people?" Isabelle asked her mother one day after they returned from Vienna. "If so, is he in hell?"

Her mother replied firmly that her mother's father had *not* gone to hell. "If he killed anyone, it would have been in self-defense."

For a time after Vienna, Isabelle repeatedly asked her parents under what conditions it was acceptable to kill another person. Worried, her mother encouraged her daughter to speak to their minister. On a Saturday morning in October, Isabelle walked the mile and a half from home to the First Presbyterian Church, where she surprised the minister by asking about John Brown. Hadn't *he* killed to end slavery? Was it moral to kill in service of a good cause?

"My maternal great-grandparents brought rifles to anti-slavery crusaders in Kansas," Isabelle said. "Was that immoral? Does our family bear that stain?"

"Brown is *sui generis*," the minister said.

"What does that mean?"

"Unique, one of a kind. He did some good, but the Pottawatomie Massacre shouldn't serve as an example for anyone."

"But was killing *necessary* to end slavery?"

"Historians will long debate that question. Our Presbyterian Church teaches that God has the power to bend evil to good. I personally believe that killing in the Civil War was necessary to end slavery. It's an example of God bending evil to good."

Isabelle's paternal grandparents had also come to Kansas as opponents of slavery, but they didn't transport weapons or ride with John Brown. William's grandfather, a businessman, built the first large volume dry-goods store in the state. William's mother died young of tuberculosis, and her pain and anguish drove her son into medicine, where he hoped to mitigate suffering. He received a medical degree from the Columbia University College of Physicians and

Surgeons in New York. Anne, whom he'd known in Topeka, was three years younger. They married shortly after she graduated from Wellesley College in Massachusetts and lived in New York while William completed his training. A photograph in their living room showed William as a young man, tall and well built, though not athletic. He had little interest in sports. Isabelle saw some resemblance in the picture between herself and her father—both were tall with the same thick, light brown hair. In the photo William is laughing at something Anne, who stands next to him, has just said. She's short with long, almost black hair. An accomplished pianist, Anne taught music at Washburn College in Topeka and sometimes performed with orchestras and bands around the state. She had a soft, inviting body, which attracted small children and puppies. As a little girl, Isabelle sometimes timed how long it took for a small person or pet to climb onto her mother's lap.

The Presbyterian upbringing of both parents mandated what they called "lives of service." This meant they were often gone, leaving Isabelle at her cousin Diane's home. Anne not only taught piano and performed professionally but volunteered for the Red Cross and other "do-gooder" organizations, as she called them, including a mixed-race group advocating the integration of Topeka's schools, libraries, and hospitals. That group had recently become more active because of the wartime "Double V" civil rights campaign advocating victory over oppression abroad *and* at home. Isabelle's father worked far more hours at the local Stormont Hospital than required. Many local physicians had volunteered or been drafted to serve in the military, and Stormont, where William was chief of surgery, was short-handed. Isabelle's mother had once said that they were "just too busy" to have a baby until their mid-30s, when Isabelle was born. Some of their neighbors had considered the late birth even more "different" than the Graham's bungalow or their membership in a group favoring racial integration.

Isabelle considered her pre-Vienna life in Topeka idyllic and recognized that her sorrow after the year abroad had cast what seemed a shadow over the household. She sensed her parents' worry that she might never be happy again. Following in her mother's footsteps, she'd attended Wellesley College, majoring in German, and writing an honor's thesis on the works of Stefan Zweig. She was a senior when Japan bombed Pearl Harbor in December 1941, bringing the United States into the war. As graduation neared the following spring, she'd requested permission from her parents to join the WAVES, the newly created women's branch of the U.S. Navy. Wellesley's president had recently become its first director. Anne and William urged their daughter to come home for a while before enlisting. They feared that military service would deepen her melancholy.

By her third week home from Wellesley, Isabelle was contributing stories to the *Topeka Daily Capital,* whose editor was a neighbor. She had run into him shortly after her return to Topeka and remarked on war-related changes in their hometown.

"Write about it for the paper," he'd said.

A year had passed since that conversation. Some subjects Isabelle chose on her own while others were assigned by editors—the arrival of POWs on the hospital train, for example. She worked part-time, which she liked, making $5 per story, $8 if the piece was especially long. Some nights, she accompanied fellow reporters to the movies, but usually she stayed home, playing cards and reading with Anne until her father returned, which was often long after supper.

On the morning after German POWs arrived, Anne drove Isabelle to the pig farm to ride Joe. They had only one car, which was shared by both parents and their daughter. Penny, cousin-Diane's horse, had been sold long before, but Isabelle's Joe still shared a pasture with Daniel Jones's mare. Bumping up the rutted driveway, Isabelle didn't see Daniel's old truck and figured he'd gone into town for coffee with friends. After getting a bridle, she stood outside the barn looking around. Rainbow colors shimmered in mist rising from the creek. Daniel—she didn't run his two names together anymore—had never married, and injuries from bronco-busting had kept him out of the war. His bad back and bum knee must have made it hard for him to keep up the farm, Isabelle realized that morning. As a child, she'd considered the place paradise, but now she noticed that two of the four stairs to the front porch were missing and several windowpanes were broken.

Coyotes somewhere nearby yapped over a kill, silencing the pigs. The sounds and sights took her back to summers before and after Vienna. When the Grahams returned home from their year abroad, Isabelle and Diane had competed side by side and sometimes against each other in horse shows and rodeos. They had both won ribbons, but their relationship had frayed as Diane's inner fire burned ever brighter and Isabelle's dimmed.

Diane skipped a year of high school and entered the University of Kansas at age 17, leaving Isabelle two years behind. After that, they seldom saw each other. A brilliant physics major, Diane published articles in scientific journals, and in early 1941, the army came for her, sending her to someplace no one, not even her parents, knew.

As Isabelle walked from the barn to Joe's pasture, the sun was burning off the mist, and the changing light took Isabelle back to the *Laternenanzünder* in Vienna who came early each morning to quench flames in lamps lining the street where the Grahams lived. Though much of Vienna had electricity by then, their street was still lit by gas. The tiny fires resisted dying, which intrigued her, as did the golden glow that lingered in fog after the flames went out.

Suddenly she was that child again, and Otto stood beside her, pushing a lock of curly black hair from his eyes so she could see his reaction as she translated something he'd just read.

In front of their house was a yard, and there stood a juniper tree. In the winter one day the woman stood beneath the tree and peeled herself an apple, and as she was peeling the apple, she cut her finger, and the blood fell onto the snow.

This won't do, Isabelle thought, forcing herself back into the present. *It hurts too much to remember.*

She had reached the rusted pasture gate, and when she pulled it open, Joe came running. He was 13 now, sleek and strong, with a reddish coat that glistened in the sun. Isabelle led him back to the barn for saddling, mounted, and rode north along the creek toward town and then west on a dirt road that took them across a limestone bridge over a creek coming out of the Flint Hills. Isabelle knew that creek merged into the stream she and Diane had often followed on Daniel Jones's farm, and a few miles beyond that confluence, the combined waters flowed into the Kansas River, which, in Kansas City, joined the Missouri, and, in St. Louis, the Mississippi. The girls had enjoyed imagining the leaves and twigs that fell into the pig farm's creek journeying the long distance to the Gulf of Mexico.

On the limestone bridge, Joe balked. He had never liked bridges. Isabelle gently coaxed him to take the first step, and after that, he kept going, breaking into an unbidden trot when his hoofs hit dirt on the other side. Isabelle guided him onto an old buffalo path that led into the hills. The familiar climb pleased him. He strained at the bit and Isabelle let him go at his own fast pace.

The prairie hummed in the warmth of the August sun. A buck and doe watched her from a grove of trees called red cedar in Kansas, but which Diane had discovered were *Juniperus Virginiana*, a member of the Juniper genus. A flock of orioles flew overhead. In a little less than two hours, they reached the hill called Buffalo Ridge where the Army had built a general hospital for injured and ill American soldiers and POWs. Joe stopped at the barbed-wire fence that surrounded the grounds, and Isabelle looked across 150 acres flattened by bulldozers and mostly stripped of wild grasses and flowers.

Before her was a cantonment-style hospital with 56 single story wards, each with a red brick veneer, set in long rows about 15 feet apart. She had read in the newspaper that besides the wards, there were two adjoining surgery buildings, four mess halls, a laundry, gymnasium, movie theater, post office, and gas station. Across the grounds she saw military police standing watch in a guardhouse at a wide gate. Isabelle began to circle the hospital from behind the wire fence. According to the newspaper, the facilities at Buffalo Ridge would have covered about 80 square blocks in town, and she figured the Army had chosen this site on the prairie at least partly to save money.

Construction of Buffalo Ridge General Army Hospital had begun in late 1942. It had opened for staff in March 1943, receiving its first patients in May. By now, early August, it housed about 1,000 patients. According to Isabelle's newspaper, it would eventually treat almost 3,000. Most would be war-injured or ill American soldiers, but military personnel and civilian employees from bases and other military installations in Kansas and surrounding states could also receive treatment there. Last night's hospital train had brought the first prisoners of war.

Through a window in a ward just inside the fence, Isabelle saw patients lying amidst the lifts and pulleys of traction. A covered walkway linked some of the buildings, making it easier for those in wheelchairs to get around. Army nurses walked in small groups along a street that circled the hospital grounds. A small detachment of soldiers assigned to the hospital marched in formation further along that street. She could hear them counting cadence. Skirting the fence, she urged Joe forward and noticed a physical therapy building, basketball court, and baseball field. The hospital was a small town, she realized, almost complete unto itself. The many buildings, though substantial, felt impermanent, as if they knew they didn't belong in that place and would vanish when the war ended.

Hearing a piano, she stopped for a few minutes near a ward with a south-facing sunroom. Through a large window, she saw a crowd of people—some sitting on the floor—listening to "Take the A Train" by Billy Strayhorn. She couldn't see the pianist, but he—or she—played expertly, Isabelle thought. After Strayhorn, she heard a jazzy arrangement of Jerome Kern's "The Way You Look Tonight."

Continuing to circle the grounds outside the perimeter fence, she noticed a ward set apart from others and surrounded by double razor wire. Two armed military policemen stood guard next to the only passageway through the wire. Spotting a nurse within shouting distance, Isabelle called to her.

"Who's in that ward?" Isabelle asked. "I'm a reporter from the local paper. Are the POWs who arrived last night confined there?"

The nurse looked where Isabelle was pointing. "I've heard that most of them left early this morning for clinics in camps around the state," she said. "Only the sickest and most injured POWs will be treated here." Pointing to a building about 40 yards away, she advised Isabelle to seek more information at hospital headquarters.

"We've been ordered not to talk about the POWs," the nurse said.

Continuing around the fence toward the only gate into the grounds, Isabelle saw a barn and wondered what it might hold. A man watching from the barn door beckoned as she drew near.

"Bring that handsome beast over here," he said, limping toward the fence. He wore a cowboy hat, plaid shirt, jeans, and, on one foot, a well-tooled boot. On the other foot were bandages and a soft slipper. At the fence, he pulled gloves from a pocket to spread the barbed wire and then reached through to rub Joe's ears and face. "What a beauty! I bet he won ribbons in shows. Was he a cow pony before you got him?"

Isabelle nodded yes to both questions. The man was tall and too thin. She saw a scar coming down from under his hat along his cheek and neck. He also had scars on his left forearm. He asked her to turn her horse in place, and as she complied, he recited,

> *When I bestride him, I soar,*
> *I am a hawk:*
> *He trots the air;*
> *The earth sings when he touches it;*
> *The basest horn of his hoof is more musical than the*
> *pipe of Hermes.*

"That's Shakespeare!" Isabelle exclaimed.

"Yes! Who said it and in what play?"

"I don't remember."

"The dauphin in *Henry V.* I'm Lieutenant Billy Greenwood. Who are you?"

"Isabelle Graham. My editor at the *Daily Capital* sent

me to report on the prisoners who arrived last night. I'm on my way to headquarters."

Billy Greenwood frowned. "Damn Krauts. I won't take them riding."

"You've got horses in the barn?"

"Yes, the docs here believe that horses are good for 'battle fatigue.' He spit the words out with disdain. That's what they call shell-shock. I call it ruination. Battle breaks brains as well as bones, and some of us don't recover." Pointing toward the guardhouse at the entry gate to the hospital grounds, he told Isabelle to meet him there. "I'll talk you past the MPs," he promised.

Billy walked slowly because of his injured foot so Isabelle took her time circling on Joe to the gate. As she approached the guardhouse, she heard Billy explain to the guards that he needed to test her horse for patients' recreational use. The MPs opened the double-sided gate and Isabelle entered the grounds before dismounting and handing the reins to Billy. Slowly they crossed a parade-ground to the two-story headquarters building, where, without asking permission, Billy mounted Joe and urged him into a trot toward the barn, soon disappearing from view.

Inside headquarters, an information officer received Isabelle, put his feet up on his desk, and, after scrutinizing her from head to toe, invited her to sit down. She asked for permission to interview POWs for her newspaper.

"I reported for the *St. Louis Post-Dispatch,* before the war," the officer responded. "You don't want to talk to those guys. They won't tell you anything. What you want to do now is have lunch with me. And tonight, we'll go to a movie in town."

Isabelle couldn't keep from laughing. He joined her but then got serious and turned down her request.

"Prisoners at this hospital are in bad shape. You can't interview them, and I doubt that will change in the future. If it does, I'll call your editor. I suppose you'd need an interpreter?"

"I speak German."

"Fluently?"

"You must be born into the language to be fluent, but I do all right. My family lived in Austria for a year, and I've studied German privately and in school ever since."

The officer's face brightened as if she'd said something marvelous. He asked if she knew German medical terminology.

"A little. My father studied surgery in Vienna and sometimes discussed cases at home. He has a fat German-English medical dictionary we could loan you."

"Would you consider interpreting occasionally for us?" We're desperate now that prisoners are arriving. The Army has already snapped up most German speakers around here."

Isabelle's reaction to this question surprised her. She felt relief, as if a long-awaited gift had finally arrived. She told the officer that he'd have to contact her editor, but with his permission she'd willingly interpret occasionally at Buffalo Ridge.

After calling an aide to give her a hospital tour, the information officer left to consult with the commander. With the guide, Isabelle toured a gymnasium where healthy young men—orderlies or "attendants" the aide called them—were playing basketball. She also spent time in a classroom where a lecture on the new drug penicillin was underway. She walked by several medical wards and an officers' mess before arriving at the guardhouse next to the razor wire fence that surrounded the POW ward. Billy was there on Joe yelling back and forth with a man with a bandaged head who stood behind an open barred window. As Isabelle watched, two MPs left the guardhouse to better hear the conversation. The strange scene struck Isabelle as unlikely to ever happen to her again.

"No, this horse is not a Trakehner," Billy insisted. "He's an American Quarter Horse. They're a mix of breeds, including Thoroughbred."

The patient indicated that he didn't understand, so Isabelle stepped up to translate. When she finished, a very large man appeared in the window. He stared for a few seconds at Isabelle and Billy and then shoved the questioner aside before slamming down the window.

"Damn Krauts," Billy swore again. He pointed at his bad foot. "One of them probably planted the mine that did that!" Then he wheeled Joe around and headed for the barn. Isabelle's guide returned to headquarters after giving her a pass that allowed her to explore alone. When she heard piano music again, she followed it until she came to the sunroom of the orthopedic ward. Standing out of the way of patients and staff entering through a screen door, Isabelle peered inside to see who was playing.

Billy came limping up behind her. "His name is Jake Newman, and he performs for us most afternoons. Like me, he was wounded by a mine in Tunisia, but on a different hill.

Maybe you know him. He's from Topeka."

Isabelle didn't know him.

"He's a musical prodigy who left home during high school to study at Julliard in New York. Want to meet him?"

She did, but not then. She had to get back to the office to file a story. Standing outside the sunroom, they listened to a Chopin nocturne for a few minutes and then went to the barn, where Joe was tied to a post. Billy pronounced him "a worthy steed" and then introduced Isabelle to the three hospital horses and his Appaloosa, Ash, who was handsome but skittish with her, a stranger.

Billy asked Isabelle how often she rode Joe.

"Maybe once a week. Sometimes not that often."

"We need another horse here. You'll be doing the injured soldiers and Joe a big favor if you let me borrow him until the war's over."

Isabelle said she'd think about it.

From the barn, she rode back out the gate to the limestone ridge that gave the hospital its name. About 70 miles north was Nebraska and below her was an ancient riverbed where Isabelle and Diane had dug for buffalo bones during their adventuring. She stopped briefly and then continued east toward town until she found the cottonwood tree that had served as a marker for Wildland. The tree had grown taller and the stick shelter was gone, but otherwise the hideout hadn't changed. While Joe drank from the creek, Isabelle looked north across miles of big bluestem and other wild grasses rippling in the wind. On the edge of her consciousness hovered shadowy memories of Vienna during the time when her tutor had disappeared. Pushing those memories far back in her mind, she left Wildland and rode Joe as fast as she dared along rutted paths to Daniel Jones's farm. His car was still gone. After unsaddling her horse and turning him out to pasture, she walked two miles to catch a bus into town. By the time she got to the office, she'd decided who to mention in her story: the prisoner behind bars who asked if Joe was a Trakehner; the injured soldier who expertly played Chopin; and the cowboy whose horses might heal the souls of wounded men. At the end of the piece, she'd inform her readers that the hospital needed her help.

"I feel obliged to answer the call," she'd write.

On her desk, she found a note ordering her to report immediately to the editor. Bounding up two flights of stairs, she entered his office out of breath. He turned toward her from a window overlooking the State Capitol.

"The hospital commander wants you back there first thing tomorrow," he said." I agreed because you'll get good stories, but don't ever let down your guard."

"Against what?"

"Use your imagination. Some of those prisoners will be dangerous."

Chapter 2

Billy Greenwood's team of doctors had conspired to keep him at Buffalo Ridge as long as possible because he was good medicine for their patients. Isabelle didn't learn this right away, but in her first week of interpreting, she heard that Billy had arrived in Topeka on the first train of wounded American soldiers. Hobbling on crutches, he had quickly identified patients who couldn't read because they were illiterate, blind, or because their burned hands couldn't hold a book. He visited wards with a backpack full of magazines like *Life* and *True Story* and also popular novels by Raymond Chandler and F. Scott Fitzgerald, among others. When asked, Billy read aloud to patients. The horses had arrived three weeks later, and, bragging that he could ride before he could walk, Billy became hospital wrangler. Red Cross volunteers trained to care for patients took over the job of reading to them.

Billy had shrapnel in his skull, abrasions on his face, neck, and arm and an infected foot from the mine-explosion in Tunisia. Surgeons had removed the small toe and a bit more of his left foot and also slivers of metal from his skull. His brain had been bruised, but hospital doctors said it was healing. They were required to send healthy men back to combat—or at least to a military desk job—but they convinced the chief medical officer to keep Billy at Buffalo Ridge as long as possible. By the time Isabelle arrived, Billy had a full-time Army assignment as assistant librarian and wrangler. He took patients and staff horseback riding almost every day when the weather was good.

On her first morning of work at the hospital, Isabelle ran into Billy while walking briskly to the prison ward with Chief Nurse Captain Margaret McGrath who was recounting where she'd served since the war began: a forward hospital in the Philippines, which she termed "a nightmare," and, after that, Letterman Army Hospital in San Francisco. Originally from Maine, McGrath had served 20 years as an Army nurse. Struggling to keep up in spite of his limp, Billy accompanied the two women to the prison ward, where an MP waited to escort them through the gate in the razor wire and into the building. Billy continued on to breakfast.

Just inside the ward, Captain McGrath explained to Isabelle that one of the prisoners, a corporal named Ernst Bauer, was adamantly refusing surgery. "He speaks only German and can't understand why an operation is necessary. He's too hurt and sick to be dangerous but watch out for the big sergeant. He's a bully—or worse."

A physician in scrubs and an orderly met them inside and led them through the building, which had separate quarters for enlisted prisoners and officers. Isabelle saw two living rooms, two kitchens, a joint library/game room, four bunkrooms, five single bedrooms, and three bathrooms. The MP said that since no officers were then under treatment in the prison ward, the eight enlisted men were using the whole building. Only two were currently there; others were undergoing medical procedures elsewhere at Buffalo Ridge.

In a single bedroom, the recalcitrant patient, Corporal

Bauer, sat in a simple wooden chair. Next to him on one side was a table, and on the other side, a hospital bed. The table held a book with a title Isabelle was too far away to read. Above the table she saw a large photograph of a bay Thoroughbred, the legendary Nero, a failed racehorse trained and ridden by Alois Podhajsky of the Spanish Riding School in Vienna. A close follower of events in Austria, Isabelle remembered that the two had won the bronze in dressage at the 1936 Berlin Olympics.

Corporal Bauer struggled to hold himself upright in his chair. Layers of gauze encircled his head; a brace and sling obscured his left arm. He tried to stand to receive the two women and, failing that, nodded deeply—almost a full bow—while seated. A large man lumbered heavily into the room and came so close behind Isabelle, she could smell him. Glancing back, she saw a boxer's flattened nose. It was the same person who'd slammed shut the window of the ward the day before.

An enforcer, she thought. *Not here to help, but to control.*

The chief nurse asked Isabelle to introduce herself to the patient, and she quickly explained in German that she would serve as his interpreter. He asked in Standard High German if she was a professional. Isabelle remembered from Otto's lessons that, among friends, German speakers might use a local dialect, but strangers often address each other in High German.

The doctor interrupted. "Tell the patient that yesterday's X-ray revealed that his humerus isn't healing. The complex fracture was clumsily set. Pieces of bone endanger the radial nerve. If we don't operate to clean up the damage, he'll lose full use of that arm and hand."

Isabelle translated the doctor's words after explaining to the patient that she was a volunteer interpreter, not a professional.

When she finished, the corporal said, "Liebes Fräulein, I hear Vienna in your diction. Tell the doctor the setting of my broken arm by a poorly trained medic at the prison camp in Tunisia was a nightmare. The pain since then has been severe. I hesitate now to undergo surgery which could prolong my pain."

Isabelle noted that the patient had recognized her accent, which could, but didn't necessarily, mean that he was Austrian. She translated the doctor's response: "You're weak from dysentery and have spent many weeks suffering severe pain. I understand your reluctance. Nevertheless, you must undergo surgery to avoid permanent damage to your radial nerve. It is my obligation to strongly urge that you do this. The pain from the operation will last only a few days. Without surgery, your pain will be chronic."

"Where were you trained?" Bauer asked the surgeon.

"The University of Michigan."

Suddenly the big man behind Isabelle shoved her aside and spoke harshly to Bauer. "Machen Sie es einfach!" he ordered. "Just do it!"

"Alles in Ordnung," Bauer responded. "Understood."

Bauer tried again to stand up, but his knees buckled. The orderly eased him onto a litter. The MP took one end and the orderly the other. The large sergeant, determined to help carry the litter, started to shove the orderly aside, but the MP barked, "Stay back! You may not leave the ward." Isabelle and the head nurse followed the patient and carriers out the door of the ward and across the grounds to the surgery center, which had a separate wing for POWs. A nurse in that wing said Isabelle needn't stay but should return in two hours. Corporal Bauer disappeared into a wing of operating rooms.

As they left the surgery center, Chief Nurse McGrath told Isabelle that Bauer had spoken only a few words since arriving at the hospital. "Besides the broken humerus, he has infected scalp wounds and amnesia from brain damage."

"What caused his wounds?"

"From what I could understand, he doesn't remember. He clearly took a severe blow to his head and arm. He also got dysentery at the camp in Tunisia. The Allies never planned for taking so many prisoners. You saw how thin he is."

"What should I do when he wakes up?"

"Translate for him. If he's in pain, tell the nurse. Be kind but keep your distance. We are not allowed to fraternize with POWs."

McGrath headed toward another ward; Isabelle continued alone to the barn where she told Billy he could pick up her horse at the pig farm anytime convenient for him. She couldn't predict her schedule at Buffalo Ridge, she said, but would help with the horses when possible. Pleased to be getting Joe, and eager to spend time with Isabelle, Billy handed her a pitchfork and together they tossed hay from a pile near the barn up into the loft. After that, they curried the horses.

Later, Billy would admit to Isabelle that he'd observed

her closely that day and concluded that she was blind to her beauty. He'd wondered if it was because she'd attended a college with no men to stare at her. Billy was 6'2 and Isabelle was, he thought, at least 5'10. Perhaps she considered herself too tall to be attractive to men? On that day she wore light brown slacks and a white linen shirt that revealed a curvaceous figure. Her shiny, brown hair was held back by a clasp at the back of her neck.

Billy asked how she'd learned German.

"From a tutor in Vienna, where we lived for a year, and from teachers in Topeka. I majored in German at Wellesley."

"Did you enjoy Vienna?"

They were currying the haunches of Billy's horse then, and Billy was surprised when Isabelle straightened up and stared at him in silence. Then she changed the subject.

"I like the German language very much. My professors at Wellesley considered me proficient, but I'm not really fluent."

"Will you find it difficult to help the POWs?"

She hesitated even longer this time before answering, "I've wondered that myself."

Billy noted her reluctance to respond to certain questions but didn't press for more information. When they finished cleaning and currying, they walked across the hospital grounds to the officers' mess where they joined a cafeteria line served mainly by Negroes. The medical staff at Buffalo Ridge was all white, as were the patients. Prisoners of war could be treated at the hospital, but not Negro American soldiers. U.S. Army policy mandated segregation of its ranks and facilities, including hospitals. Isabelle had heard the hospital segregation policy might change when more Negro soldiers took part in combat, but for now, they had their own hospital in Texas. At Buffalo Ridge, Negroes cooked and served meals, did laundry, cleaned facilities, and cared for the grounds. Isabelle was not surprised by any of this—she'd grown up in racially segregated Topeka; but, like her parents, she opposed it.

A soldier called loudly from across the room, "How'd you get such a babe, Greenwood?" Within seconds that patient and two others were dragging their chairs to Billy's and Isabelle's table, miming that Isabelle had stolen their hearts. They pretended to push Billy off his chair, and he laughingly resisted. The interlopers used napkins to dry imaginary tears before returning to their tables. Like most of the patients in the mess, they wore green pajamas under red corduroy robes.

"Those men are in worse shape than you might think," Billy said. "In my experience, if a soldier complains of pain, it's usually a ten on a scale of one to ten."

After lunch, Isabelle returned to the surgery center where she found Corporal Bauer propped up with pillows and sipping orange juice in a recovery room. He was very pale. His arm was covered with bandages, which, according to the attending nurse, would soon be replaced by a cast. Before leaving the room, the nurse showed Isabelle a button attached to the bed. "Press it and a light will blink at our desk," she said.

Bauer spent some time studying his interpreter. "I accept that the surgery was necessary and am grateful to you and the surgeon," he finally said.

Isabelle asked how he felt.

"Tired and nauseated from whatever they use to kill the pain."

"Would you like me to read to you?"

"You called yourself eine Freiwillige earlier. What does that mean in this hospital?"

"In English the word is volunteer," she said. "I'm a reporter for the local newspaper and came yesterday to write a story about the POWs. When the information officer learned that I speak German, he asked me to try interpreting. I couldn't say no."

Bauer said that since he'd arrived at the hospital no one had spoken his language well enough to explain why surgery was necessary. "That's why I refused. I will request that you alone translate for me from now on."

He looked at her quizzically and asked why her German had "hints of Vienna."

"As a young girl, I lived there for a year. A tutor instructed me almost every day in your language."

"Interesting," Bauer said. "Are you a spy?"

Surprised, Isabelle at first said nothing. She wanted to know why he'd think that, but recognizing his fatigue, said simply, "No, I'm just an interpreter."

Bauer removed a pillow with his one good arm and lay flat. Pointing at a book on the table, he asked Isabelle to read to him. The book was the same collection of Stefan Zweig's novellas taught in Isabelle's advanced German seminar at Wellesley. She paused for a moment to recall her encounter with the great writer in Vienna. Otto, her tutor, had been right about Zweig going into exile. After failing to feel at home in London and New York, among other places, Zweig and his wife had died together by suicide in Petrópolis, Brazil, on February 22, 1942.

All of that passed through Isabelle's mind as she picked up the book and chose the novella *Angst* to read aloud in German while translating silently for herself.

> *Als Frau Irene die Treppe von der Wohnung ihres Geliebten hinabstieg, packte sie mit einem Male wieder jene sinnlose Angst... As Irene came down the stairs from her lover's apartment, that senseless fear suddenly gripped her again. All at once a black spinning top began buzzing before her eyes, her knees froze in dreadful rigidity, and in haste she had to catch hold of the banister rail to avoid falling headlong forward. It was not the first time she had dared the risky visit; this startling tremor was by no means new to her.*

Corporal Bauer fell asleep before she finished the first page. Sitting quietly with the book in her lap, Isabelle again saw Stefan Zweig rise in the Café Landtmann to praise Otto for teaching "The Juniper Tree."

It occurred to her for the first time that the fairy tale had meant far more to her tutor and Stefan Zweig than she had understood. By February 1934, both men surely foresaw what lay ahead. Zweig was fleeing harassment by the anti-Semitic, fascistic Home Guard in Salzburg. Her tutor belonged to a left-wing group, Republikanischer Schutzbund, the Protection League of the Social Democratic Workers'

Party. Both men suspected by then that their world was on the verge of destruction, which explained why Zweig so effusively praised the last paragraph of "The Juniper Tree." The family at the dinner table symbolized a broken world put back together again. The murdered boy, magically transformed into an instrument of vengeance, had killed the wicked stepmother by dropping a millstone on her head. Now Isabelle recited those words in English to herself.

> *The father and Marlinchen heard this and came out: there were steam and flames and fire rising from the place, and when that was over, the little brother stood there, and he took his father and Marlinchen by the hand, and the three of them were so happy and went into the house and sat down at the table, and ate together.*

Otto Maurer had disappeared from Isabelle's life shortly after the encounter with Stefan Zweig in the Café Landtmann. Now Isabelle sat in the recovery room of a U.S. Army hospital with an injured soldier asleep beside her who, she thought, might be Austrian. She had searched for Otto on the streets of Vienna, on the train to France, on the ship to America, and even at rodeos and horse shows in Kansas. Surely, he would find her and explain why he'd left without any explanation. Her parents had offered confusing reasons for his disappearance, and because she feared their answer, she'd resisted questioning them closely.

Had Otto been killed in the Februarkämpfe, the short Civil War that broke out in Vienna the same month they met

Stefan Zweig? Even now she couldn't admit that possibility so she forced herself to concentrate on the book in her lap. The coincidence of the titles of the three novellas with her own feelings made her smile: *Fear, Burning Secret, Confusion.*

The surgeon and a nurse soon arrived to examine Bauer, who woke up complaining of pain in his wrist and lower arm. The surgeon turned to Isabelle and requested that she ask for a more specific description. "If it's a *piercing* pain, it means something different than a *dull* pain," the surgeon said. Isabelle translated that for Bauer, and he chose "dull" to describe what he felt. The doctor said he thought the pain would soon ease. Bauer immediately argued that Isabelle's ability to distinguish between dumpf (dull) and stechend (sharp) indicated the importance of gebildet (erudite) interpreting in a medical setting. He asked that only Isabelle interpret for him in the future.

Isabelle saw the surgeon struggle to contain his ire. An enemy prisoner—perhaps a man responsible for the injuries of Americans dying at the hospital—was making demands? Who did this corporal think he was?

"I have just met Miss Graham," the doctor finally said. "I believe she works here only occasionally. She does not live at the hospital."

"I will make a formal objection to the Red Cross if an interpreter assigned to me is less competent than Fräulein Graham," Bauer said in German, and after Isabelle translated, he continued, "The lives of us prisoners depend on the skill of the translator."

The surgeon asked Isabelle to follow him into the hall.

"I don't like to admit it, but he's right. Would you consider working here full-time?"

Surprised again by a feeling of anticipation—of doors suddenly swinging open—Isabelle told the surgeon that she'd long sought a way a way to be useful during the war and would be grateful if the Army hospital used her skills full-time. "My editor will have to agree, and I'll want to be trained as a nurse's aide. That way I can help our own soldiers as well."

The surgeon said that wouldn't be a problem. "The Red Cross is running regular training sessions for aides here. However, the commander must sign off on this. I'll speak to him. Go straight to headquarters when you leave here."

Isabelle returned to Bauer's bedside and read *Angst* aloud for an hour until he slept again. Then she summoned a nurse and left for headquarters, where the hospital commander began their conversation with a question about Bauer.

"What do you think of him?"

"I don't know him well enough to say."

"You don't find him presumptuous?"

"He may be accustomed to getting what he wants."

"He was way out of line with the surgeon, but it worked. If you agree, we'll hire you as a civilian employee. We need all the help we can get. You'll receive a salary to live here and be available day and night. The Red Cross will quickly train you as an aide. I phoned your editor and told him we need you as a matter of national security."

"National security?"

"You'll be interpreting for enemy prisoners. Though we

don't actively spy on them here, their conversations interest us. Perhaps when interpreting, you'll learn something significant and share it with us. Do you have a problem with that?"

"I'll let you know if I do."

"How did you get to the hospital this morning?"

"By bus."

"In an hour my assistant will be free to drive you home. Return here at 0730 tomorrow morning. I'll get someone to watch over the demanding corporal until then. Leave your belongings at the nurses' quarters when you arrive tomorrow and report immediately to the Surgery Center."

"Lieutenant Greenwood wants my horse in his barn."

"We'll take care of it. That is all, Miss Graham."

Outside headquarters, Isabelle heard piano music again and followed it to the sunroom of the orthopedic ward. Though she tried to enter quietly, the screen door slammed loudly behind her. Jake Newman didn't flinch at the noise. He sat askew on the bench, his wounded right leg sticking out to the side and pedaling with only his left foot. He was practicing scales on a handsome upright with a rich tone.

Patients at tables around the room were playing games. Isabelle noticed canasta, casino, and chess. They continually razzed each other, a way of keeping fear and sorrow at bay, Isabelle figured. She sat down in a chair between two of the tables.

After running scales, Newman played chord inversions, stopping occasionally to leaf through charts like those used by Isabelle's mother. Isabelle had studied piano but never excelled. Jake Newman was short and trim. He wasn't handsome, Isabelle thought, but he was sexy. When he looked up for a few seconds and noticed her, he raised an eyebrow and flashed a roguish smile. She blushed and, to hide it, picked up a newspaper. The Wehrmacht had recently failed in a major offensive around Kursk in Russia, giving the Red Army an important victory. The reporter quoted an analyst who claimed that the tide of war was turning. The possibility made Isabelle dizzy with relief, and at the same time, filled her with dread that it might not prove to be true.

More patients and staff filed into the sunroom, which reminded her of a private club—plush rug, book-filled shelves, piles of newspapers and magazines. A woman with casts on an arm and foot entered on crutches—mortar injuries incurred at a forward hospital in Tunisia, Isabelle would later learn. A man sitting near the door gave his chair to a patient whose eyes were covered by bandages. The orderly who'd led him into the sunroom sat down nearby. A doctor in scrubs took a place on the floor directly in front of Isabelle. He looked so tired she thought he might lie down and fall asleep at her feet. Several patients came into the sunroom from beds down the hall—a man on crutches who'd lost part of a leg below the knee and two men in wheelchairs, their laps covered by blankets. Perhaps they'd each lost both legs; she couldn't tell.

Billy Greenwood entered the sunroom and waved at Isabelle but stayed back by the screen door. Isabelle found him attractive but a bit skittish, like an overgrown colt. She figured the nervousness was related to his brain injury. People kept arriving in the sunroom until there was nowhere to sit, even on the floor. Sunshine streaming through tall, south-facing windows lit Jake Newman like a theater spot. Without introduction, he began the concert with "Paper Doll," a current hit, playing it sweetly—like the Mills Brothers sang the song on their record. After that, Jake ran through an arrangement of music from *Oklahoma* and *Pal Joey*. He spoke the lyrics from "What Is a Man?"

> *What is a man?*
> *Is he an animal?*
> *Is he a wolf,*
> *Is he a mouse?*
> *Is he the cheap or the dear kind?*
> *is he the champagne or the beer kind?*
>
> *What makes me give?*
> *What makes me live?*
> *What is this thing called man?*

Newman scooted back on the piano bench and rising awkwardly because of his bad leg, said, "No applause, please." He spoke almost in a whisper. The audience leaned forward to hear him.

"Private First Class Clyde Sloane arrived here two weeks ago. Wounded on an island half a world away, he died last night. I visited him before his death and felt what the poet Walt Whitman wrote many years ago,

> *...poor boy! I never knew you,*
> *Yet I think I could not refuse this moment to die for*
> *you, if that would save you.*

No one spoke after that. Newman played the first movement of Chopin's "Sonata #2 in B-Flat minor," the "Funeral March," a piece Isabelle had heard her mother perform. When he finished, he sat with his head lowered as people filed quietly out of the room.

After everyone had left, Isabelle introduced herself. Newman said that his father, a French-horn player and professor of music at the University of Kansas, had occasionally performed with her mother. They walked together down a hall that ended in a large room filled with patients in traction. Jake stopped outside a door just before that. "My leg isn't healing properly. I run a low fever most of the time, which makes me tired. I'll sleep now and hope to see you another day."

Chapter 3

At home later that afternoon, Isabelle packed a suitcase and placed it by the back door where her parents would enter the house after work. It was a small, brown suitcase that brought back memories from Vienna and Wellesley. Aides at Buffalo Ridge wore uniforms, so she'd packed only pajamas, cowboy boots, jeans, underwear, two blouses, a sweater, and two skirts. Her parents stopped and looked skeptically at the suitcase when they came in the door. Isabelle briefly explained why it was there, and with a glance of mutual understanding, her mother and father insisted on waiting until after dinner to discuss her move. They'd had busy days and were hungry. Anne sent Isabelle into the garden to pick whatever looked good for a salad.

The sun was low in the sky, but it was still hot—maybe close to 100. Isabelle sat on the back steps in the shade of the house, trying to relax. Her parents' reaction had made her think. Had she decided too precipitously to move to Buffalo Ridge? When asked by the surgeon, she'd immediately said she was willing. Why? The word *redemption* came to mind, raising still more questions. Did working at the hospital offer a way to *repay* or *rescue* herself or another person? Why think of *redemption*, a word steeped in religion? As the sun set and rivers of red and gold ran through the sky, she picked two cucumbers and a green pepper and then went back inside. Dinner was tense, which was unusual, and when they finished, Anne asked the first question.

"Is it wise to work closely with German prisoners of war, given your experience in Vienna?"

Isabelle posed her own question. "What about that experience should make me turn down a job that helps the war effort?"

William answered: "The Februarkämpfe, civil war, in Vienna was traumatic, Isabelle. It led to Otto's disappearance, which darkened our lives. At first Anne and I thought you mourned the absence of his company, but it went deeper than that. We've never discussed this, and perhaps we should have, but you came face to face with evil at a very young age. It left you melancholic, which you hadn't been before. Why immerse yourself in more sorrow now?"

The term "face to face with evil," disturbed Isabelle. To exactly what evil had she come close? She decided to ignore it. She did not want to think about the events of the short war that had broken out that February in Vienna. She told her parents that she felt guilty working at the newspaper.

"As we speak, men I might have married are dying in battle. I have an obligation to do more than write features for the *Daily Capital.*

Anne pressed her case. "The work at Buffalo Ridge could be dangerous. POWs trying to escape might take you hostage."

"The prisoners at the hospital are wounded and sick," Isabelle said. "When they get better, they're moved to guarded camps around the state. I understand your concern, but today I was offered a useful wartime job, which I want to accept. Please don't remind me that Buffalo Ridge treats enemy prisoners and not Negro American soldiers, which I agree is wrong. The U.S. Army needs interpreters. They need *me* now, and I *will* answer the call. In fact, they want me at the hospital early tomorrow and I'll be grateful if one of you will drive me. Your support will keep me on an even keel."

Isabelle's parents knew better than to throw a damper on their daughter's new-found enthusiasm, and at first light the next morning Anne drove her through the gates of Buffalo Ridge and helped her move into the nurses' quarters. The room had only a narrow bed, lamp, chair, and tiny closet with one small shelf.

A "nun's cell," Anne called it.

For two days after his surgery, Corporal Ernst Bauer slept most of the time, which left Isabelle free to study the Red Cross manual for nurses' aides. On the third day, with support from two orderlies, Bauer returned to the prison ward. Each day for a week after that, a physician or nurse came to check on his arm and head wounds. Isabelle interpreted and also asked questions as a way to educate herself. How severe were his wounds? Why were pins inserted into his arm?

Ten new ill and injured German prisoners arrived at the hospital during the week after Bauer's surgery, and Isabelle also interpreted for them. Most left within a day or two for clinics in one of the closely guarded camps around Kansas. At night, Isabelle got on-the-job training to be an aide. She liked her teachers—a Red Cross nurse and an older Army nurse who reminded Isabelle of chief nurse Captain McGrath.

When Isabelle had time, which wasn't often, she joined Billy Greenwood in taking patients riding in the Flint Hills. On those occasions she met American soldiers with "psycho-neurological" conditions, which she found interesting. Had the trauma of battle physically altered the brains of those men? Would they recover? Billy told her about a patient who hadn't spoken a word since arriving at the hospital. "I can tell he's a farm boy," Billy said. "He's familiar with horses and eager to help in the barn. Does silence somehow provide refuge from his pain? I don't know and neither do the docs."

Isabelle received her aide certificate on a Wednesday during the third week of August. By then she was busy 12 hours a day, seven days a week. Besides interpreting, she drew blood, changed bandages, gave bed-baths, and helped turn disabled patients over in their beds. She saw and smelled gangrene and consoled a soldier weeping over the amputation of his foot. She provided the new drug penicillin to sufferers of syphilis and gonorrhea, apparently occupational hazards of soldiering.

At the end of August, the hospital commander called her into his office to confirm that she would stay indefinitely.

"As long as I'm needed," she said.

"What is your opinion now of Corporal Bauer?

"He has less pain in the arm and has gained some movement in that hand. His amnesia persists. He's eating more and putting on a little weight."

"What else do you know about him?"

"He seems well educated and has good manners. I would say that he was raised to be a gentleman."

"Can you tell where he's from?"

"I believe he's Austrian."

"Some nurses think he's an imposter."

"An imposter?"

"They believe that he's only pretending to be a corporal. He's more accustomed to *giving* than *taking*, orders," they say.

"Why would a prisoner of war pose as someone he's not?"

"Good question. Some imposters hide their identity to avoid being charged with war crimes. Others have information to sell but are waiting for the right moment to do it. That may be Bauer's motive. Keep your eyes and ears open."

On the last night of August, Isabelle awakened to the sound of footsteps and voices outside her bedroom window. In the dim light she saw orderlies carrying litters. She learned the following day that those patients—all Americans—had to be removed from a hospital train through windows. Their condition was too fragile to risk lowering them down stairs. As they passed Isabelle's window, someone cried out in pain, which took her back to Vienna. She didn't sleep the rest of that night.

Chapter 4

B y the second week of September the prison ward at Buf-falo Ridge held three patients besides Corporal Ernst Bauer: the bully, Sergeant Hermann Schneider, and a private named Manfred Müller, both of whom had severe hepatitis, and also another private, Erhard Schmitt, who suffered from life-threatening malaria and spent most of the time in bed. Isabelle seldom interpreted for those men because each spoke enough grade-school-level English to carry on simple conversations with doctors and nurses. One day she over-heard Private Müller and Sergeant Schneider discussing in German the first national celebration of Adolf Hitler's birth-day in 1939, when he turned 50. Schneider described march-ing in a "glorious" parade in Munich with fellow members of the Nationalsozialistische Deutsche Arbeiterpartei—the Nazi Party. Müller said he'd done the same in Ulm, his hometown.

Because of his accent, Isabelle was almost certain that Corporal Bauer was Austrian. When she asked him about it, Bauer claimed not to know. To Isabelle, he seemed almost a different species from other prisoners who came through the ward. Bauer was formal and polite with nurses and physi-cians who treated his injuries. He often said that Isabelle had saved his life by correctly interpreting the doctor's explana-tion of why surgery was necessary. One day, overhearing that praise, Sergeant Schneider yelled in German that Bauer was "fraternizing with the enemy." Isabelle reported the outburst to the hospital commander, who immediately called in Captain Brian Freeland, who led Buffalo Ridge's detachment of Military Police. Isabelle repeated what she had told the commander and added, "Sergeant Schneider moves through the ward like a small tank, so I usually know where he is. He'll run water in the kitchen, pretending to be washing dishes, but he's actually just outside the living room eavesdropping on Bauer and me."

Freeland explained that Nazi prisoners of war had long-standing orders from party superiors to exert strong control over fellow POWs wherever they were. He'd heard about suicides and beatings in camps of prisoners who had been accused by hard-liners of turning traitor. Perhaps Schneider and Müller suspected that that Bauer was a potential stool pigeon. Freeland told Isabelle to alert the guards outside the prison ward if she ever felt in danger.

By the beginning of the third week of September, Isabelle was working even longer hours. Buffalo Ridge was short of staff because the Army kept transferring doctors, nurses, orderlies, and aides to hospitals assembled elsewhere in the United States from where they would eventually be moved to Europe or Asia. There were rumors that planning was underway for the invasion of Europe, which would explain why so many physicians and nurses were sent east from Kansas.

Billy and Jake each invited Isabelle to movies in the hospital theater and to lunch or dinner in the officers' mess. Older and more experienced with women, Jake serenaded her on the piano and enticed her into storerooms to make out, but he never went further than that. He said he felt awkward with his bad leg. Billy, whose injuries were healing rapidly, showed no such constraint and wooed Isabelle with poetry, a powerful aphrodisiac. On a rare horse-back ride alone together, they watched across the prairie as the sun dropped beneath the horizon.

Billy recited Rainer Maria Rilke:

Lord: it is time. Summer was truly grand.
Over sundials cast your shadow now,
in the open fields let loose the winds.

Demand fullness from the last ripening fruit;
and add on for them two warm days,
urge them to mature and chase
last sweetness into heavy wine.

Whoever has no home now, will build none.
Whoever is alone, will be so for much longer,
will stay awake, read, and write long letters,
will restlessly wander up and down avenues
when the leaves are blown about.

Back at the barn, Billy led Isabelle up the ladder to the hayloft. Their horses snorted and pawed in the stalls when they heard unfamiliar cries from their keepers. At Wellesley, after Pearl Harbor, Isabelle and three of her friends had decided to shed what they considered the "burden" of virginity. They'd had no trouble finding young men at nearby colleges who felt the same.

"That was one positive by-product of the war," Isabelle

said when she revealed to Billy that she'd been with another man.

On September 16, a Thursday, Isabelle went early to the prison ward to interpret for the psychiatrist and neurologist who had been treating Ernst Bauer's brain injury since his arrival at the hospital. It was their weekly visit to check what they considered severe amnesia.

The psychiatrist began with the usual question: "Do you remember how you got injured?" Bauer thought for a few seconds and then said that he could see himself "falling through fire." Isabelle observed that the memory surprised him.

"I've never seen that image before," he said. I must have woken up on the ground because I remember reaching for meine Erkennungsmarke—dog tag—but it's gone. Without it I'm lost, a non-person. I can't remember who I am, which is terrifying. I vaguely remember being carried by fellow soldiers to a prison camp near a big city. At some point the name 'Corporal Ernst Bauer' must have come to mind. I don't know if it's actually my name."

The specificity of these memories pleased the physicians, who considered them a sign that Bauer would most likely fully recover his past. He still suffered from the lingering effects of dysentery and wore a brace on his injured arm, but he had regained almost full use of that hand.

At times, Isabelle felt like Bauer's servant. He was polite but didn't hesitate to ask her to do chores for him, which reinforced her opinion that he was accustomed to being served by others and especially by women. Sometimes she caught him staring at her, but he always kept his distance.

One day be asked for an easel, paper, and paints, and she brought them to him from the office of the occupational therapist.

His favorite subject to paint was Nero, the horse in the photograph on the wall of his room. An Austrian-American Red Cross volunteer had given Bauer the photograph at Halloran Army Hospital on Staten Island, the first place he'd landed in the United States. In his paintings, Bauer imagined Nero as ein fliegendes Pferd, a winged horse soaring above the hospital. Isabelle asked why he made Nero a horse who could fly, and Bauer gestured to the bars on the window of his bedroom, where they were painting.

"I hope I never become accustomed to imprisonment."

He continued to suffer from blurred vision and sometimes asked Isabelle to read aloud. They had argued over Zweig's *Angst*. In that story, an angry husband sends a blackmailer to scare his unfaithful wife into submission. She has little money to pay for silence and considers suicide to escape her predicament, but in the end, she returns to her husband and children.

Isabelle found the husband sadistic. Bauer agreed that the husband was unnecessarily cruel to seiner untreuen Ehefrau, his unfaithful wife, but argued that using a blackmailer was the only way to save the family, a noble goal.

On September 25, she was reading aloud another of Zweig's novellas, "Burning Secret," when Bauer interrupted her.

"I admire the writing of Stefan Zweig but find him personally verwerflich, reprehensible," Bauer said.

"Why verwerflich?"

"Because he fled Austria when he should have remained in the country to resist the Nazis. In exile, he committed suicide, a sin in my religion."

"What is your religion?"

"Catholic. I no longer believe in God, but I live by a moral code engrained in me as a child. And, by the way, that moral code makes me question the values of your country. I know that Buffalo Ridge and other hospitals in this city are racially segregated, as are your libraries, schools, movie theaters, restaurants—too many places to name. I also know that Adolf Hitler praises America's racial policies. They influenced his despicable treatment of Jews, as you've no doubt heard."

Isabelle waited a few seconds before responding because she hoped Bauer would keep revealing details of his past. When he remained quiet, she told him about her parents' civil rights work and their abolitionist background. Then she asked, "Where and by whom were you taught your moral code?" Bauer started to respond but caught himself. "It taxes my strength to look back. Please don't ask me about it."

Chapter 5

The day after Bauer criticized Stefan Zweig, Isabelle rapped on Jake Newman's door in the orthopedic ward to say she'd be serving as an aide there for a while.

Jake's leg had mostly healed but would never bend again. Doctors kept him at the hospital because he still ran a fever. He often helped fellow patients, and when Isabelle knocked, he had just returned from assisting someone in traction. Frowning, he blocked the doorway so she couldn't enter.

"Please check immediately on Lieutenant Nolan in bed 11. His temperature is 103 and rising," Jake said.

"What wounds?"

"Smashed leg and arm—machine-gun fire. No cast on the arm because of swelling from infection. If it's cellulitis they might amputate."

"Should I come get you if he's taken to surgery?"

"Yes, bang hard on the door. I was up much of the night and want to nap now. Please let Nolan know that his parents will arrive this afternoon."

"Where's home?"

"St. Louis."

Finding Lieutenant Nolan awake and burning with fever, Isabelle smoothed his sheets and asked if he felt like dancing. He smiled and said he did. She told him his parents were on their way and asked what he needed.

"I'll be grateful for a glass of juice and a sponge bath."

For the next hour Isabelle sponged cool water over Lieutenant Nolan's burning body—wherever she could reach without hurting him. She was especially gentle when she bathed his grossly swollen arm.

He surprised her by asking where he was. "I know it's a hospital in Kansas, but where?"

"Just west of the capital, Topeka. If you could get up and look through that window, you'd see a ridge that drops into miles of open prairie. In a nearby barn are handsome horses for you to ride when you feel better. You can ride *my* horse down Buffalo Ridge. The path leads to a gully where we'll look for buffalo bones. They'll make good stories for your children."

"I've never ridden a horse and don't have a wife or children."

"There's a first time for everything. My horse is patient with beginners. A nurse I know, a good rider, will come with us. After the war, you'll marry her and have three children."

"Why not you?"

"She's prettier and will make a better mother."

Isabelle sat with him until another patient requested help, and while she tended to him, orderlies came to carry Lieutenant Nolan to the surgery center. He was gone before his ward mates could send him off with the usual banter. Isabelle ran to get Jake, who as quickly as he could with his stiff leg, followed Nolan. Jake hated the idea of fellow patients facing surgery alone. Isabelle stayed behind, turning men in their beds, and adjusting their traction. A private who looked younger than 18, the age on his chart, beckoned her to his bedside and said he'd traveled to Kansas on the same train as Lieutenant Nolan.

"He was hurting bad on the trip. Will he survive surgery?"

Isabelle said she didn't know. She had learned not to lie to wounded soldiers.

"Well, maybe it would help if I sing 'We'll Meet Again,'" the boy suggested. Without hesitating, he began the song in a pitch-perfect voice that brought whistles of appreciation from around the room. Some of the patients in the ward knew every word. Others hummed, but everyone participated in some way. Windows were open, and the men sang loud so Lieutenant Nolan could hear them before being anaesthetized. At the end, the private spoke the words, "I know we'll meet again. I *know* we'll meet again."

While waiting for Jake's return, Isabelle sat between the beds of two patients in traction and read aloud a story from the *Saturday Evening Post* in praise of an American soldier's heroism in Italy. One of the patients had lost his left arm below the elbow; both hands of the other man were burned and covered with bandages. Isabelle was still reading when Jake limped back into the ward and asked for help wheeling patients to the sunroom. He didn't mention Lieutenant Nolan. The singing youngster had fallen asleep, and Isabelle didn't wake him. In the sunroom, Jake ran through chords and finger exercises on the piano.

Isabelle went to the ward canteen and ate a meager lunch by an open window. The air outside was warm, the sky a cerulean blue.

Soon Jake played the notes of his first song. He did it with one finger, and at first, she didn't recognize the music.

When he added chords, she realized it was an improvisation of "We'll Meet Again," his way of informing ward-mates that Lieutenant Nolan was gone.

"He died of sepsis from cellulitis in his arm," Jake said later, tears running down his face. "The doctors tried very hard to save him."

That afternoon, Isabelle worked in the orthopedic ward until she was no longer needed. Then, back in her quarters, she sat on the bed and obsessively recalled each detail of her encounter with Lieutenant Nolan: the feverish brightness of his eyes; skin almost too hot to touch; the question about where he was being treated.

How sad that no one had thought to describe where he was dying!

In her mind's eye she saw his parents pull into the hospital parking lot and hurry to headquarters where they ask to visit their son. The receptionist calls the hospital commander who leads them to the surgery center, where a physician gives them the terrible news. Isabelle sees the lieutenant's mother try hard not to weep, but she soon breaks down, as does her husband. The body hasn't gone to the morgue yet, the doctor says, and Isabelle imagines the parents' anguish as, for the last time, they embrace their beloved son.

Isabelle knew she should pay her daily visit to the prison ward but felt paralyzed, caught between death in the present and dark memories from the past. Depression and street violence had frayed the fabric of Viennese life when Isabelle and her parents lived there. She vividly remembered hearing a well-dressed gentleman at a table in the Café Central explain to friends that he wouldn't see them the following morning because he could no longer afford even a *Franziskaner,* an espresso with whipped cream.

Adolf Hitler, an Austrian by birth, had been appointed chancellor of Germany the year before, and Isabelle and her tutor eavesdropped on rancorous debates in cafés about the new chancellor's intentions. Would he intervene in the country where he was born? How dangerous was his anti-Semitism? One morning at a café in the Prater Park, a Jewish violinist much admired by Otto described being attacked by *Grobianen*—ruffians. The violinist repeated anti-Semitic slurs shouted by his assailants, and dismayed, Otto refused to translate the words for Isabelle.

Sitting on the bed in her nun's cell, Isabelle remembered the paramilitary forces, almost gangs, struggling for dominance in Vienna's streets and heard again the ringing of the telephone in their apartment early one morning. Isabelle's father had answered the phone. It was Otto calling to say he couldn't come to teach German that day. His home, the Karl-Marx-Hof, a massive public housing complex built during the period when the Workers Party led the municipal government (there was also a George-Washington-Hof), had been attacked by the *Heimwehr*, an armed right-wing organization. Otto's group, the social democratic *Schutzbund*, was vigorously resisting, but Austrian soldiers had set up light artillery and were preparing to attack. Isabelle's father said he heard gunfire in the background. The call ended quickly with Otto promising to phone again in the afternoon.

William and Anne wanted to buy a newspaper with more information, so the three of them walked to a nearby café. Inside, the atmosphere felt charged. Isabelle wouldn't have been shocked to see sparks fly through the air. At the table next to them, a young man read aloud from that morning's *Arbeiter Zeitung,* the newspaper of the Social Democrats. Isabelle interpreted what she could understand for her parents.

The day before, in the city of Linz, the right-wing Heimwehr had forcibly searched the headquarters of the Social Democratic Workers' Party, and members of that group, the Schutzbund, had resisted. Since then, street fighting had spread through Linz and other cities. In Vienna, leaders of the Schutzbund had barricaded themselves in the public housing. The two sides exchanged small arms fire during the night. The newspaper article, which had gone to press late the night before, confirmed that martial law had been declared and regular troops were gathering outside the Karl-Marx-Hof and other places.

When the student finished reading, no one at his table spoke. Isabelle's father said, "We should return to our apartment in case Otto calls."

All day they waited for the phone to ring. They sometimes heard breaking glass and shouting outside but never saw soldiers or guns near their apartment. At about eight that evening, someone knocked on the door. When her father opened it, Isabelle was surprised to see Otto in a jacket that looked wet from rain, which was strange because it wasn't raining. When he came inside, she saw that the jacket dripped blood.

"Soldiers shelled the Karl-Marx-Hof," he said. "They used tear gas to force us out into the streets, where they shot us. My parents stayed in the apartment; I don't know if they survived. I believe meine Wunde is not serious, but the bullet must be removed. I can't go to a hospital—they're arresting anyone who arrives with injuries. Please help me, Dr. Graham."

Anne stepped in front of Isabelle then so she couldn't see what happened next. Herding her like a lamb through the hall to her bedroom, Anne ordered her daughter to go to bed, but it was too early for sleep. Disturbed by what she'd seen, Isabelle sat for a long time looking out her window at the gas streetlamps flickering in the wind. The fragile flames sometimes disappeared only to bravely pop up again. *They don't want to die,* Isabelle thought.

The next morning, after a night of what she thought were bad dreams, Isabelle asked her parents what had happened after they sent her to bed. Her father said that he had performed minor surgery to remove a bullet that hadn't penetrated far into Otto's back, and he had then returned home to find his parents. William and Anne, exhausted from being up most of the night, deflected other questions. Looking back now, Isabelle saw that they had been as shocked and dismayed as she was by Otto's bloody appearance at their apartment. He was their friend as well as hers. Isabelle's father had also said that Otto couldn't tutor anymore because of his role in the uprising, which made no sense to Isabelle. Afraid of the answers, she asked no more questions.

Of course, her father was hiding something. But *what*? An Austrian soldier had shot her tutor in the back. That was the only fact she knew for certain. Did another soldier shoot Otto dead when he returned to the Karl-Marx-Hof?

Now, she *must* return to the present and visit the POW ward. Every week, new prisoners arrived—German and, increasingly, Italian, who had their own interpreter. Most POW patients didn't stay long at Buffalo Ridge, but they often needed immediate interpreting. Isabelle ran across the hospital grounds to the ward and was relieved when Corporal Bauer said she wasn't needed. That night she skipped supper, fell asleep early, and dreamed that a Laternenanzünder, lamplighter, turned from his work to glance up at her window in Vienna. It was Diane, her light-obsessed cousin. The dream woke Isabelle up, and she wept into her pillow, crying for Lieutenant Nolan and for Diane. Would she disappear as Otto had done, never to be found again?

One day at the end of September, Jake Newman came into the mess where Isabelle was eating lunch and asked her to accompany him to the prison ward. He wanted to urge its patients to audition for a talent show. He hoped to entice at least one POW into playing a major role on stage to attract attention from reviewers at important newspapers in Kansas City, Chicago, and New York, who surely would cover an Army Hospital show featuring a POW and written by a pianist who, before the war, had made a name for himself in

New York.

When they reached the ward, a military policeman came out of the guard house and escorted them to the door. He said he'd remain inside the protective razor wire fence in case they needed him. Accustomed to Isabelle's frequent visits, the guards paid little attention when she came alone.

Inside, she heard the sizzle of something frying. The bullying sergeant was cooking in the kitchen. Bauer sat alone in the living room. Isabelle introduced Jake as the *Piano-spieler,* and Bauer turned to him with delight, standing to shake hands and praising Jake's musical skills.

"No matter the weather, when you perform, we open the window to listen," Bauer said, with Isabelle translating. "I especially admire your interpretation of Schumann. I heard you practicing his piano Concerto in A minor the other day. It's one of my favorites."

Pleased by the praise, Jake explained that he was producing a talent show and would soon hold auditions for anyone at the hospital.

"That includes the Negro workers," Jake said. "It also includes you."

Bauer laughingly disavowed any musical or dramatic talent, but the malarial prisoner, Private Schmitt, heard them from his bedroom and came slouching into the living room in a robe and pajamas. He stood for a moment looking around and then announced in barely decipherable English that he was an "almost famous" tenor in Cologne.

In German, he said, "I lack the strength to perform before an audience, but with your permission, I will gladly sing now a *Kunstlied* by the Austrian, Hugo Wolf. As you may know, the lyrics are by Joseph von Eichendorff."

Jake said he'd like that very much, and Schmitt sang *Verschwiegene Liebe*, "Secret Love," with a resonance and power that brought patients and staff to their windows, which banged open across the hospital grounds.

Over treetops and pastures
Into the glorious light—
Who may guess them,
Who could catch them?
Thoughts swaying to and fro,
Secret is the night.
Thoughts are free.

If only she could guess
Who has thought of her
In the whispering groves
When no one is awake
Only the clouds flying fast—
Secret is my love
And beautiful as night.

When Schmitt finished, Bauer exclaimed loudly, "Was für eine Schande! So eine Schande! What a shame! You should be on stage, mein Freund, not imprisoned in a foreign land. I well remember taking a tram from near our home in Währing to the Theater an der Wein, where Richard Tauber was performing. He sang 'Verschwiegene Liebe.' Your voice reminds me of his."

Hearing the outburst, Sergeant Schneider came running

from the kitchen. Had Bauer said something revealing? Perhaps the fact that he'd lived in Währing, a prosperous district of Vienna? Did Schneider doubt Bauer's proclaimed identity? Jake poked Isabelle then to continue translating, and he questioned the opera singer about his career. Schneider returned to the kitchen. When Private Schmitt went back to his room, Isabelle and Jake left the ward.

The next day a messenger intercepted Isabelle on her way to the orthopedic ward and said MP Captain Freeland wanted to see her in his office.

"Have you learned anything more about Corporal Bauer?" Freeland asked.

"He's Catholic, and yesterday he mentioned that he'd lived in the Währing district of Vienna and had attended a concert at one of Vienna's finest theaters. He considers Stefan Zweig 'reprehensible' because he fled into exile instead of staying home to fight Hitler and also because Zweig committed suicide in exile."

Freeland said he'd learned the day before that the branch of American Military Intelligence—he called it "MI"—charged with interrogating POWs was looking for an amnesiac Viennese Luftwaffe major who'd been shot down over North Africa and might be a prisoner in America.

"Based on what you've told me, Freeland added, "I'll urge MI to send an agent immediately."

Chapter 6

Three days later, over lunch in the mess, Jake Newman told Isabelle that a "jackass" had interrupted his concert the day before.

"I'd just finished 'String of Pearls' and 'Day Dream' when I felt something change in the room. A stranger came in with no scars or missing limbs. Ramrod straight and radiating privilege, he stood out like a sore thumb. He interrupted my break, saying he was U.S. Army Captain Stephen Yost. No one else has ever bothered me during a break. He claimed we'd met before the war in a New York club where I was performing, but I don't remember him. He asked a question that made me see red: 'Why'd you enlist in the infantry when you could have entertained the troops?'"

Isabelle understood why the question disturbed Jake. He'd joined the infantry as an enlisted man to avoid taking advantage of his talent and privilege. "I was about to swear at the jerk, but he kept talking," Jake said. "He claimed to be vetting interpreters at prison camps, but he's higher up the chain of command than that. The lie really burned me. I elbowed him aside and pounded out 'Praise the Lord and Pass the Ammunition.'"

Jake's description of the intruder unsettled Isabelle. Surely, he was the spy from Military Intelligence. He'd come to Buffalo Ridge because of information she had provided. Suddenly, she felt afraid for Ernst Bauer.

After lunch, an MP came to take her to Captain Free-land's office. A stranger rose when she entered the room; he had to be Yost, the MI agent. Jake had described him well—tall, robustly healthy, confident. Speaking fluent German, he asked Isabelle to tell him everything she knew about Ernst Bauer, which she did—also in German. Bauer had remembered falling out of the sky, she said. His head injuries had mostly healed but were serious enough to explain his amnesia. He had lived in the Währing district of Vienna.

Then, switching to English so Captain Freeland could understand, she said, "Sergeant Schneider should be removed from the prison ward. He is increasingly hostile towards Bauer."

Yost frowned, perhaps offended that a mere interpreter would make such a demand.

"What do you mean, 'hostile?'"

"Hateful. He treats Bauer like an enemy."

Yost got up from his chair and went to a window that looked out over the hospital grounds. Isabelle sensed his mind whirring. He had a German name and spoke the language as if he'd been born into it. An American since birth, though, she figured, and the product of very good schools. He had a sprinter's body—thin and wiry. His hair was cut short, and he wore tinted glasses. She couldn't see the color of his eyes. When he turned around again, he surprised her by saying something complimentary.

"You've done a good job, Miss Graham. Unless you sense imminent danger, let's stick with the status quo. Moving Sergeant Schneider might upset our target in a way we can't anticipate."

"Target?"

"Yes, Bauer is a target. We're spying on him now, or, rather, you're doing it for us. We think he's about to turn— to offer strategically useful intelligence in exchange for something from us, maybe settlement in this country or the extraction of someone back home. Behave no differently with him than before. We'll order MPs to pay extra close attention when you're in the ward. I'll work from an office in hospital headquarters, and you will report to me every day. That is all, Miss Graham."

Disturbed by the conversation, Isabelle left headquarters and walked through the front gate to Buffalo Ridge, where she stood for a long time looking across the ancient riverbed at seemingly endless prairie.

She marveled at the life-changing power of war. She was now officially spying on a man who might be a Luftwaffe officer. Her friends, Jake and Billy, continued to suffer lingering effects of combat. Staff turnover at the hospital was punishingly rapid because of planning for the invasion of Europe. At least that was the explanation most often offered for staff shortages. Nurses who helped train Isabelle as an aide had suddenly left several weeks before. Where were they now? She thought of Allied leaders like General Eisenhower, who had grown up in nearby Abilene. He was planning an invasion in which tens—no, *hundreds*—of thousands of soldiers and civilians would die. Did the so-called corporal, Ernst Bauer, have information that could prevent some of those deaths?

From the ridge she went back through the gate to the barn to find Billy. They'd ride together, and perhaps make love, which would soothe her anxieties. He was on the roof, caulking leaks. She called to him and watched as he awkwardly descended the ladder. Though the foot wound had healed, he was still unsteady.

They rode a rough path west of the hospital, trusting their horses to avoid rocks and brambles. She and Billy had become so close that silence between them was comfortable. As they rode side by side across the Flint Hills, Billy recited Lewis Carroll.

> *There was a young lady of station.*
> *"I love man," was her sole exclamation.*
> *But when men cried, "You flatter,"*
> *She replied, "Oh! no matter.*
> *Isle of Man is the true explanation."*

On that ride, Billy talked about himself, which was unusual. His great grandparents, like Isabelle's, had come to Kansas as abolitionists, and his parents, also like hers, had attended college in the East. Billy had chosen the University of Kansas so he could meet people from around the state in preparation for his future as a cattleman. It was all he'd ever wanted to do. An English major, he'd excelled in his K.U. classes. In the Army, he'd led a platoon in a battle for a crucial hill in Tunisia. Ten of his men had died on that hill, and now he recited to Isabelle not only their names but also their hometowns.

After a while, they dismounted and led their horses along the trail. "I'm worried about Ernst Bauer," Isabelle said.

"Why?"

"He doesn't behave like a corporal. Military Intelligence has sent a spy to discover his identity. I'm afraid for his life."

"The prisoners in this hospital have posed multiple dangers from the beginning. Your corporal is no exception."

Isabelle asked, "Do you have a gun in the barn?"

"I have a .45 Colt semi-automatic brought from home because of rattlesnakes. It's hidden among bandanas in my old saddlebag, which is hanging from a hook near Ash's stall. Why do you ask?"

"Maybe I'll need it."

"Do you know how to use it?"

"Yes. My high school boyfriend's idea of a good date was to shoot beer cans down by the Kansas River. I can hit a can from 50 feet."

The next morning, Ernst Bauer and Isabelle were painting in the prison ward when, suddenly, Bauer announced that images from his past were dramatically appearing in his mind

"They develop like a photograph," he said, "indecipherable at first and then becoming clear. I'm recovering myself."

His lower arm was still protected by a brace, but he made good use of his hand. His hair, which was dark brown, had grown back. He had very blue eyes. Female aides and nurses found him irresistible. They flirted, and Bauer flirted back. He seemed so comfortable with women that Isabelle figured he must have a sister. He knew classical music and knowledgeably critiqued Jake's piano performances. He and Isabelle often debated the merits of their favorite authors. He liked Hölderlin and Goethe, while Isabelle preferred Zweig and Thomas Mann.

Ernst Bauer confused Isabelle. He was almost certainly an Austrian soldier. An Austrian soldier had wounded—perhaps killed—Otto, her tutor. Bauer remembered falling through fire, which indicated he might be the missing Luftwaffe pilot sought by Military Intelligence. If so, he had no doubt shot down Allied pilots, maybe even someone Isabelle had known during her years at Wellesley. Two men she dated from Harvard had joined the Army Air Corps. Now, painting with Bauer in the prison ward, Isabelle admitted to herself that she had, over the years, fantasized avenging her tutor's sudden disappearance. No, she thought now, Otto's sudden *death*. Though she wasn't sure, she suspected that her father hadn't been able to save Otto. That would mean Austrian soldiers were responsible for Otto's death, so why was she feeling *protective* of Corporal Bauer, who was surely Austrian? Not only protective, she felt a moral obligation to keep him alive.

In a rare moment when she was sure Sergeant Schneider wasn't eavesdropping, she casually told Bauer that she'd heard him mention that he once lived in the Währing district of Vienna.

"I thought that would interest you," he responded. She took it as an invitation to probe further.

"Did you live near the Vienna Woods? If I remember correctly, they border Währing."

"When I look back, I don't see woods."

"Did you have a horse?"

"Maybe. The horses here feel—smell—familiar to me. I'm healthy enough to ride with you now." He paused for a few seconds, as if he had to make up his mind about something before continuing.

"Can you get permission to take me riding?"

Something had changed. He was open, decisive, and clearly wanted to get her alone. She sensed he had more to say but couldn't do it in the ward. He was still weak so taking him on a prairie trail would be risky, but they could ride on the hospital grounds. The weather was perfect, cool and clear. She suggested they go to the barn as soon as she asked his physician for permission. Bauer agreed. It took her about an hour to find the doctor, who cautioned her to ride slowly with Bauer because his arm was still healing. After that, Isabelle went to MP Captain Freeland's office. He wasn't there, but she told an aide what she was about to do, assuming he would brief Agent Yost, who had gone out but was due back soon.

From headquarters, Isabelle went to the barn to alert Billy. At first, he insisted on accompanying her and Corporal Bauer. Isabelle refused. "Schneider, the big sergeant, is the problem, not Bauer," she told Billy, who, after a heated discussion, agreed to prepare the horses if she'd ride where he could see her and Bauer at all times. He didn't mention the pistol, and she didn't consider taking it with her. From the barn she went to her quarters and changed into riding clothes. She didn't feel nervous. Nor did she feel in control. There was no turning back from what had been set in motion.

In jeans and cowboy boots, she hurried to the prison ward and wasn't surprised when Sergeant Schneider opened the door, his heavy body blocking Bauer, who stood helplessly behind him.

"He can't ride with you. It would be too dangerous," Schneider said.

Isabelle disingenuously praised Schneider for his concern. Then she insisted that Bauer's mental health would benefit from proximity to a horse. "Perhaps you'd like to ride with me another time," she told Schneider. "We could go tomorrow and gather bones."

That piqued his curiosity. "Bones?"

"Yes. Earlier prairie inhabitants drove buffalo off the ridge that gave this hospital its name. We'll go tomorrow morning. You needn't worry today about Corporal Bauer. You'll be able to see us most of the time."

Schneider hesitated and then stepped aside. Bauer and Isabelle left the ward.

Isabelle rode Ash and Bauer rode Joe on a saddle with a safety harness invented by Billy for injured patients. Because of his still-weak arm, Bauer needed a boost onto Joe, which Billy provided. He also fashioned a sling and secured Bauer's brace so it wouldn't bump against the saddle horn.

Bauer laughed at the contraption and said, "Jetzt haben Sie mich gefesselt!" "You've got me shackled!" Taking the reins in his stronger hand, he moved them gently to the right and left, practicing neck reining, which reminded Isabelle that European riders usually hold a rein in each hand, pulling one individually to turn the horse's head. On the periphery road, Bauer addressed Joe as if he were a child. "Gut gemacht, guter junge," he said repeatedly, "That's good, good boy."

Watching him ride, Isabelle found Bauer regal despite the ungainly saddle. Sitting straight and tall, he handled Joe gracefully. Their mounts walked briskly, ready to trot or canter at the slightest urging. Bauer kept looking up and exclaiming, "Was für ein riesiger Himmel! What an immense sky!" When a cardinal sang from trees beyond the fence, Bauer whistled the same song. At the northern edge of the hospital grounds, Isabelle stopped so they could look out over the prairie. "Wie der Ozean, ozeanisch—like the ocean, oceanic," Bauer observed.

After circling the hospital twice, they returned to the barn, where Billy helped Bauer dismount. After that, Billy left. Isabelle would later learn that for a while he'd stayed close enough to hear Isabelle if she called for help. Bauer went from stall to stall in the barn, running a hand up and down noses, necks, and flanks. The horses seemed grateful for his touch. *He must have had a horse as a boy,* Isabelle thought. She was currying Joe when Bauer came into the stall.

"As a child I figured I'd have a lifetime with horses, but the Bundesheer, the federal army of Austria, made me into a pilot, and I became addicted to flying. Nothing except airplanes has mattered much since then."

Isabelle tried to remain calm.

"When did you join the army?"

"In 1933, just before the February Uprising. You lived

in Vienna then, I believe."

Bauer, Joe, the stall—everything—disappeared. Otto Maurer stood before Isabelle, his coat wet with blood.

She asked Bauer if he'd shot protesters in the uprising.

"No, I had just begun my training outside the city."

"Have you only pretended to be a corporal?"

Bauer hesitated so long before responding that Isabelle feared she'd shut him down. Then he whispered to himself, "At last, it begins." After that, his demeanor changed. "I am a major in the Luftwaffe," he said with pride, "a fighter pilot well known for many kills—what we call ein Experte and you term an Ace. We must speak briefly now because Sergeant Schneider will panic if I'm away too long. I have information the Allies will want."

"You faked amnesia?"

"I was shot down and lost my memory until recently."

"Do you speak any English?"

"Almost none."

"Is your real name Ernst Bauer?"

"I won't reveal that yet."

"Does Sergeant Schneider know who you are?"

"When I disappeared, an order from the Luftwaffe to search for me may have been circulated in Tunisian prison camps. Perhaps Schneider saw or heard that order. In any case, he has long guessed that I'm not a corporal named Ernst Bauer, but I don't think he is yet certain who I am."

They stepped out from the stall, and Isabelle made a quick decision. "You're no longer safe here. We must flee together on my horse."

"I won't leave the hospital until I have some assurance

that whoever extracts me has the power to grant my demands. Is such a person here?"

"Yes—an officer from Military Intelligence recently arrived."

"So, you've been spying on me from the beginning?"

"No. I came to the hospital as an interpreter. Military Intelligence became interested only recently."

"Tell the officer to bring MPs to extract me tomorrow while you're riding with Schneider. He has crude weapons hidden in the storage room and will kill rather than let me go. Do not try to remove me from the ward if he's nearby. I want you to know that I was never a Nazi. The Luftwaffe recruited me from the small air branch of the Austrian army when I was young, and I loved flying too much to defect."

He paused briefly before continuing and then spoke decisively, "Thank God I got shot down!"

"What do you want in return for information?"

"I will reveal that only to the person who can make it happen."

Isabelle stood frozen for a long moment. Should she force him to leave immediately? But how? She could threaten him with Billy's nearby gun, but Bauer would guess it was a hollow threat. Perhaps he knew best. He had never seemed afraid of Schneider. Now Bauer watched apprehensively until Isabelle nodded that she would do as he wanted. They left the barn and walked to the prison ward, which was eerily deserted. At the door, Isabelle called for Schneider to remind him about their riding date the next morning, but no one answered. Bauer walked through empty rooms and, peering out a window, said he didn't see MPs in the guard house. "Perhaps they escorted my wardmates to a movie or game room. That's happened before. You can leave now, Isabelle."

She left him behind in the ward.

Walking quickly to headquarters to report that Bauer had revealed his identity, Isabelle replayed their conversation in her mind. She heard Jake playing the Blues in the orthopedic ward. Suddenly, she knew for certain that she'd made a terrible mistake. Schneider and the other POWs hadn't gone to the movies or a game room. They were hiding—perhaps in the prison ward storage room—and they'd do that only if they meant to harm Bauer. She didn't see Billy anywhere, and there wasn't time to look for him. She sprinted to the barn, grabbed the pistol from the saddlebag, and ran as fast as she could back to the ward.

Chapter 7

Months later, after Isabelle had begun her own investigation of the events of that afternoon, Billy gave her a written account of what he'd witnessed, beginning with Isabelle and Bauer leaving the barn and walking across the grounds to the prison ward.

The two of you disappear into his ward. I go briefly to my quarters and, about 20 minutes later, return to the barn. I'm mucking stalls and feeding horses when I hear a sound that takes me back to Hill 109 in Tunisia—moaning, cries of agony. You appear at the barn door, your hair, your face, your clothes covered in blood. I move to help, but you gesture wildly for me to stay away. Emergency sirens are wailing. The hospital is locked down.

You go into Joe's stall, wipe your face with a saddle blanket, bridle Joe, jump on his bare back, and run him out of the barn. I mean run. You're headed for a low point in the fence, which Joe jumps.

Surely the POWs are to blame for whatever has happened. I'm desperate and reach into the saddlebag for my pistol, but it's gone. I quickly saddle Ash and ride him as fast as I dare across the grounds, yelling at the guards to open the gate. Circling back toward town, I find and follow the hoofprints of your horse.

Maybe an hour later, coming down from the hills, I see Joe standing over your body. I've seen too many bodies splayed out like yours. They were dead but thank God you're breathing. I go to you and feel for wounds and broken bones. Your face is smashed, your head beaten and bruised. Drying blood cakes your shirt and jeans. I try to think straight. It can't all be your blood. Some of it must have splattered from someone else. I wonder how you could have gotten back-wounds that look like someone stuck you with nails.

Terrified, I try to get my bearings. I'm having trouble making sense of what I see: the young woman I love, blood-ied on a perfect fall afternoon; birds darting among grasses swishing in the autumn wind. Your eyes are open, but you don't speak or move. We're far from a telephone. I must get you to a hospital. I pick you up and drape you gently over my horse. Then I grab a rope from my pack and tie your horse to mine. Maneuvering you into a sitting position in front of me, I hold tight and ride to a house on the edge of town. The telephone operator at the hospital puts me through to the commander, and soon an ambulance arrives, followed by a jeep with a medic and MPs. They assess your condition and load you onto a stretcher, which they slip into the am-bulance. Your father will meet the ambulance at the hospital where he works. Siren blaring, the ambulance leaves me be-hind. I ride back to Buffalo Ridge and return the horses to their stalls. I search for my pistol in the barn; It's nowhere to be found.

Word of a bloody attack in the prison ward spread quickly that evening from hospital headquarters to the office of the U.S. Provost Marshall General in Washington, D.C., and from there to the office of the commander of the U.S. Army's Seventh Services Division in Omaha, Nebraska. He listened closely to the telephone call from an aide to the

Provost Marshall General and then dialed Captain John Clevenger, the senior officer in the base's Criminal Investigations Division, and ordered him to drive to Topeka early the next morning to find out "what the hell happened."

"Two POWs are dead," the commander had barked into the telephone, Clevenger would later recount, "and two others are injured—one of them a female civilian interpreter. Makes the Army look terrible. An officer from Military Intelligence will meet you tomorrow at noon outside Stormont Hospital in Topeka."

"Military Intelligence?"

"Yes. They have an interest in the prisoner who survived."

Clevenger left Omaha before dawn the next morning and drove south through the valley of the Missouri River to Kansas City, where he turned west to Topeka, arriving in time for breakfast at a downtown cafe. After that, he easily found Stormont Hospital, a handsome three-story brick building on a tree-lined street about ten blocks from the cafe. Walking up the sidewalk to the doorway, he saw a man sitting on a bench with his head in his hands—the MI officer, Clevenger guessed. They shook hands, so alike in demeanor they might have been related. Captain Stephen Yost introduced himself, apologizing in advance for being exhausted and perhaps incoherent. He said he'd stayed close to the prison ward all night to make sure the crime scene wasn't disturbed. MPs at the front door eyed the two men warily. The Buffalo Ridge killer might still be at large.

Yost told Clevenger that the interpreter, Isabelle Graham, had fled the hospital on her horse.

"Her horse?"

"Yes, one of the horses used for recreation at the hospital was hers. The other survivor of the attack, Corporal Ernst Bauer, is near death in the hospital. He was removed on a litter from the storage room of the prison ward. The scene was ghastly: pieces of flesh, blood on the walls and floor."

"Why were you at Buffalo Ridge?" Clevenger asked.

"Military Intelligence got word that a patient calling himself Corporal Ernst Bauer might actually be a downed Luftwaffe major. I arrived a few days ago. The two dead prisoners were committed Nazis. They may have suspected that Bauer was an imposter about to turn stool pigeon."

The MPs frisked Yost and Clevenger before allowing them to enter the hospital. Clevenger went immediately to a payphone to call a forensic expert at the University of Kansas. They'd meet later at Buffalo Ridge. Yost waited for Clevenger and then the two of them went into Dr. Graham's office. White faced and exhausted, Isabelle's father nonetheless spoke with authority. "You can't visit her," he said. "She may die, and I don't want you to be the last people she sees."

"What are her injuries?" Clevenger asked.

"Last night I assisted a fellow surgeon in performing a craniotomy to relieve pressure on her brain. He also reset occipital bones broken by heavy blows. We flushed and stitched puncture wounds on her arms, back, and legs. We believe the attacker beat her with nails pounded into a bat or board. We fear infection. She's semi-conscious."

Clevenger asked what that meant.

"Her eyes are open, and her brain is functioning, but she

can't speak or move. We don't know how much she understands."

Clevenger said he sympathized with Dr. Graham's determination to protect his daughter but had strict orders from the highest levels of the Army to interrogate her. "Two prisoners of war are dead, and another may be dying. We have to know what happened."

"She won't remember anything for a long time, if ever."

"Your daughter was wounded while serving her country. She's a brave young woman and would want us to pursue this investigation."

"Is she a murder suspect?"

"I just arrived and have no suspects."

Relenting, Isabelle's father led Clevenger and Yost out of his office and up three floors to a long hall with rooms on both sides. A nurse came out of a door where another MP stood guard. Dr. Graham asked the nurse if there had been any change in his daughter's condition.

"She's stable," the nurse responded.

"You have five minutes," Dr. Graham told the two men. "I'll wait in the hall."

Isabelle lay in a bed under a white cotton blanket. Clear fluid dripped through a tube into a vein in her arm. Bandages covered her head, leaving her eyes barely visible. She stared at a fixed spot on the ceiling. Yost stood by a window and watched what happened next.

Clevenger kneeled close to the patient, and almost whispering, introduced himself as the lead Army investigator of the deaths at Buffalo Ridge.

"Please tell me what happened yesterday in the prison

ward."

Isabelle didn't speak or move. Clevenger took her hand in his and asked her to squeeze if she knew who had killed the two prisoners and wounded her and Corporal Bauer. Her hand remained limp. Clevenger said he'd try again the next day.

In the hall, he asked her father if Isabelle had ever discussed her work at the hospital.

"We spoke only occasionally," Dr. Graham said. "They kept her busy late into the evenings, and by then she was too tired to talk on the telephone. The only phone in the nurses' quarters was in the hall so she couldn't say anything confidential anyway. Her mother and I met her twice at the hospital for lunch. Isabelle praised the hard-working staff and said she liked her work."

"Did you worry she might be in danger from the POWs?"

"A parent never stops worrying. Isabelle had wanted to serve in the WAVES, but we discouraged her. She felt useful at the hospital and didn't mention being afraid."

From Topeka, Clevenger and Yost drove separate cars west to Buffalo Ridge where MP Captain Freeland led them to the prison ward. He explained that one of the prisoners, Private Schmitt, had been in the surgery center for a minor procedure when the attack occurred.

"For his own protection, we've moved him to a clinic at a camp a few hours from Topeka," Freeland said.

Clevenger objected. "He shouldn't have been transferred until I'd interrogated him. Also, why am I seeing notices on bulletin boards that claim emergency sirens sounded *mistakenly* yesterday because of an altercation in the prison ward? *Altercation*? Why are you playing down the attack?"

"To avoid panic among patients and staff. Another train with POWs will arrive soon."

As they neared the prison ward, two men came running from headquarters. The elder man carried a satchel and the younger man a camera and tripod. Dr. Owen Lattimore, who called himself an explorer in the new field of forensics, was 55 with hair that needed a trim. A medical doctor, he taught chemistry at the University of Kansas and was obsessed—his word—with using the tools of science to solve murders. The photographer was one of his graduate students.

At the gate through the razor wire fence, Lattimore sent Yost to the surgery center to check on Corporal Bauer, whose injuries would be photographed later. "The fewer people who come inside now, the better," Lattimore said. He, the photographer, Captain Clevenger, and MP Captain Freeland entered the prison ward and stood for a while observing the hallway that led to the storage room. After some time, Lattimore ordered the photographer to take pictures of bloody footprints up and down the hall.

"This isn't good. Several people have been through here."

He removed paper slippers from his satchel. The men put them on over their shoes and walked past the prisoners' living quarters down the hall to three narrow stairs that led down to the storage room. It was about 20 x 20 feet with new floor-to-ceiling shelves that Freeland pointed to as the source of weapons used in the so-called "altercation."

"The shelves were recently built, and we think carpenters mistakenly left behind boards and nails," he said.

Lattimore sat down on the steps and asked the others to join him in silently observing the scene.

Clevenger had investigated murders, but none had prepared him for the scene in front of him. He struggled not to be sick. Blood had pooled on the floor and splattered—along with pieces of flesh—on the walls. Two bloodied bodies lay on the floor. Captain Freeland identified the large man lying on his stomach as Sergeant Schneider. The smaller man lying face-up was Private Müller. A board studded with nails lay near each of them, and between them lay a Colt .45. A far wall was covered with bloody handprints, and Clevenger wondered if Corporal Bauer had been forced against that wall before being bludgeoned to the floor.

After a while, Lattimore nodded to the photographer, who tiptoed around the room taking pictures. When he finished, Lattimore walked equally carefully to the Colt .45 Semi-Automatic and, with gloved hands, lifted it from a pool of blood. The photographer snapped pictures of the weapon from several angles, and then Lattimore wrapped it and placed it in a compartment of his bag. After that, he held up the studded boards for photographing.

Inviting Clevenger to join him, Lattimore then squatted by Schneider's battered body. The two investigators compared what they observed. The back of Schneider's head had been smashed by what Lattimore termed an "instrument used as a mace." Schneider's upper back and shoulders showed similar wounds. When Lattimore turned the body over, Clevenger saw where two bullets had entered near the heart.

A coroner would rule later on the cause of death. Private Müller's smaller body lay closer to the stairs. He'd been shot twice but not beaten. The photographer took pictures of both bodies.

Lattimore asked Clevenger and the photographer to sit down again on the steps. Now, working alone, the forensic expert measured objects in the room with a tape and magnifying glass, among other tools, making notes in a small book. He also examined and measured footprints. Sometimes he requested that more photographs be taken. He gave Clevenger a roll of paper and asked him to draw the room and everything in it. When Clevenger had finished, Lattimore added pliers that he'd noticed on one of the shelves.

After four hours, the men returned to headquarters to release the bodies for removal to the morgue. Freeland said the city coroner would come the next day to perform autopsies. Seemingly indefatigable, Lattimore, followed by his assistant and Captain Clevenger, headed across the hospital grounds to visit Corporal Bauer in the ICU.

The patient lay comatose. Agent Yost was no longer there. A physician briefed Lattimore on Bauer's condition and raised his hospital gown to reveal bandaged wounds to chest and back. Bauer's head was bandaged; only his eyes were visible. They were open, like Isabelle's. The wounds of Bauer and Isabelle were similar, Clevenger observed.

"The work of a sadist," Lattimore said.

Clevenger asked the attending physician how much damage Bauer had sustained.

"He was badly beaten in the head and around his liver, which is barely functioning," the doctor said.

When the photographer finished documenting the wounds, he and Lattimore left the hospital for a hotel in Topeka. They would observe the autopsies the next day. Photographs would be developed the day after that.

Clevenger had no appetite for dinner but accompanied Yost to the officers' mess. On a wall, was another "altercation" notice, and again it made Clevenger angry.

Chapter 8

Two weeks later, Isabelle woke up in her room on the third floor of Stormont Hospital. In pain and frightened, she was desperate to learn what had happened.

"Why am I here?" she asked. "Who did this to me?"

Her father recounted what he knew.

"You fled the hospital on your horse after being attacked in the prison ward. Billy Greenwood found you near death in the hills between Buffalo Ridge and Topeka. Two prisoners were killed, and another sustained severe injuries. A Captain named John Clevenger from the Criminal Investigation Division of the Army in Omaha visited you here five times, but you never woke up to talk to him."

"Did the prisoner named Ernst Bauer survive?"

"I heard that Army Captain Stephen Yost moved Ernst Bauer from Buffalo Ridge to a hospital back East."

Billy and Jake visited Isabelle separately most days. Clevenger had interrogated them, and they'd gleaned information from his questions.

Corporal Bauer had injuries similar to Isabelle's, Billy said. They'd both been beaten by a board studded with nails. Someone had shot Sergeant Schneider and Private Müller with Billy's Colt .45.

Isabelle remembered taking the gun from the barn but nothing after that. In those early days of consciousness, she didn't think or speak clearly.

"It feels like the attack happened to someone else," she

said more than once.

Jake explained that doctors had informed the investigator, Clevenger, that neither Bauer nor Isabelle was likely to recover memories of events in the prison ward and whatever they did remember might not be reliable. The damage to their brains was that serious.

"Clevenger did a thorough investigation with the help of a forensic expert," Jake said. "The county coroner performed autopsies. But no one who investigated could say for sure who had killed whom that day. Clevenger left here deeply disappointed, but I figure the Army was relieved."

Isabelle asked why the Army would be relieved.

"There have apparently been similar attacks in prison camps around the country. POWS have tormented and even killed fellow prisoners suspected of providing information to the enemy. They have felt compelled to do that by their training, and German military law may even permit it. The Red Cross has been pressing our Army to better protect the prisoners in camps. The brass doesn't need distractions or bad publicity now as it prepares to invade Europe, so it *must* have been a relief to so neatly sweep the Buffalo Ridge killings under the rug. At the hospital, word spread that an altercation in the prison ward had led to the transfer of some POWs, and most people figured you accompanied them as an interpreter."

Isabelle listened closely to Jake, understanding only some of what he said. It took two months for her to recover enough to go home, where she continued to suffer from extreme fatigue and poor balance. She tiptoed around the house slowly in those early months, moving from one piece of furniture to the other. Her legs hurt day and night because muscles had been punctured. She fell frequently.

Bitter about the bloody events at Buffalo Ridge, Jake and Billy requested—and quickly received—medical discharges from the Army. They often visited Isabelle, who, though glad to see them, lacked the energy for even short conversations. Billy spent long hours sitting quietly with her. When Jake came, he mostly played Anne's baby grand piano in the sunroom. In mid-November, he told Isabelle that he'd perish if he didn't return to New York, and a week later, he was gone.

In the following months, Isabelle spent much of every day in bed watching cardinals tend nests in leafless trees outside the window of the upstairs sleeping porch in their bungalow. Each day she heard one train after another clatter through Topeka. The newspaper said that large numbers of men and equipment were headed east for eventual deployment from England. When Isabelle felt strong enough, Billy drove her to the tracks where they waved at the passing cars. The boys—and many were just that—looking out windows of the train reminded Isabelle of the young private who had serenaded Lieutenant Nolan at Buffalo Ridge when he lay dying.

As the weather warmed in the spring of 1944, Isabelle grew stronger. By mid-June she could sit at a picnic table and help her mother sort vegetables from the victory garden.

The back yards of houses along that side of Greenwood Street opened onto an alley where Diane and Isabelle had played as little girls. The alley had felt mysterious, semi-wild, a place in town where snakes and other prairie creatures could hide.

On this afternoon she heard the gate to the alley creak open. Neither Isabelle nor Anne paid much attention because children from the neighborhood often came through that way to weed and do other chores in return for produce. But a tall stranger, not a child, stood in the gateway. It took a few seconds for Isabelle to recognize her cousin. Two years had passed since they'd seen each other. Diane stared for a long while and then ran to gently embrace Isabelle. "I should have come before. I'm so sorry I couldn't get a furlough until now," she said, running words together in her excitement. Tightening her grip to prevent Isabelle from falling, Diane studied the scars on her cousin's arms and face. "I've seen worse ones disappear," she said.

At first the three of them—Anne, Isabelle, and Diane—discussed the weather, as Kansans often do. A thunderstorm the night before had brought welcome relief from summer heat and had also delayed the arrival of Diane's airplane at the Topeka Army Air Field.

"Arrival from where?" Anne asked.

"London. Nothing dangerous or especially exciting, but I'm not allowed to tell you more."

Her younger brothers had recently joined the Navy, she said, and were grateful for postings as ship engineers on bases in Oahu and Key West. Diane would spend a week in Topeka, sleeping at home with her parents. She hoped to see

Isabelle every day.

Diane helped Anne weed the garden and pick a basketful of beans and then supported Isabelle up the few stairs to the kitchen. Anne went to her piano, and Diane poured tall glasses of iced tea she'd found in a pitcher in the refrigerator. As when they were children, Diane took charge. She observed that Isabelle could barely follow the thread of the conversation. Diane asked if Joe still boarded at Daniel Jones's pig farm.

"Yes, but I don't ride anymore," Isabelle said.

Diane sensed the deep disappointment of that statement but said she longed to ride again and especially now, after a cooling storm. Isabelle nodded that she was willing to accompany her cousin to the farm. Diane drove the Graham's Buick. Isabelle sat quietly with her eyes closed. Riding in a car made her dizzy.

Billy Greenwood had returned Joe to Daniel Jones's farm a few days after the attack at Buffalo Ridge. Since then, Isabelle had visited Joe once and found the experience too unpleasant to repeat. She couldn't stand up long enough to brush or caress her horse, let alone mount him. Surely Joe missed her attention, she told her mother. "I fear I'll never be able to ride him again."

When Daniel saw Isabelle and Diane bumping up his driveway, he ran to the barn for a bridle, and then, arm in arm, the three of them went to the pasture to get Joe. He came trotting when he heard the gate open, and Diane, nimble and strong as ever, swung up on his back. Daniel bridled the horse and then helped Isabelle make her way slowly down to the creek while Diane exercised Joe in the pasture. Later, as Joe nibbled grasses by the muddy water, the cousins reminisced with Daniel about their early days of adventuring.

Daniel revealed that he'd been especially lonely when they first brought their horses to his farm. The Depression had left him without a job, and injuries from bronco busting left him worried about the future. His purchase of the pig farm and the arrival of Isabelle and Diane had brought relief from misery, he said. He had always thought of the girls as family.

He surprised Isabelle then by asking if she remembered anything about the attack at the hospital. He hadn't mentioned it when she visited before. Why was he asking out of the blue now?

Isabelle said she remembered nothing.

"When you first went to work at the Army hospital and the wrangler came to pick up Joe, I considered refusing to let him go," Daniel said. "I was afraid POWs trying to escape would run Joe to death. I sometimes rode the paths near Buffalo Ridge to check on him. Did you ever notice me?"

Isabelle said she hadn't.

"I saw the wrangler a couple of times riding with our own boys, not POWs, and Joe looked good," Daniel said. "That wrangler was alright, but the hospital was potentially dangerous because of the prisoners. You must have known that."

Confused and not wanting to talk about Buffalo Ridge, Isabelle didn't respond, and Daniel didn't mention the hospital again.

The next morning at the Grahams' bungalow, Diane arrived in time for pancakes, sausage, and soft-boiled eggs. Anne served the eggs with the top of the shell lopped off, which Diane considered "very English." On the feeder outside the window of the dining room, birds of almost every color fought over sunflower seeds. William and Anne sat at either end of the table, and Diane observed that they treated Isabelle as usual—no special attention or looks of concern. Diane guessed that they shared her own optimism about Isabelle's eventual recovery.

After breakfast, Anne left for work at the college. Still sitting at the table, Diane asked Isabelle what she most feared when she thought about the attack.

"That I shot the two prisoners."

"How much do you remember?"

"Only getting Billy's gun. I must have used it."

"Trauma-related amnesia—or perhaps permanent memory loss from brain damage. I've learned about both in my work. Didn't you also suffer some kind of trauma in Vienna? I remember asking you about it."

"You said I'd gone dark then. I'm darker now."

"Unresolved mourning poisons the soul."

"What do you suggest?"

"Nothing for now. You're still too weak and ill."

That was their only conversation about the killings.

In the following days, the cousins helped Anne in the garden, played Go Fish and other simple card games, and took short walks. About her own posting, Diane said only that the Army had loaned her to British intelligence. After a week in Topeka, she flew out of the Army Airfield for a destination she didn't reveal.

In the following months, as Isabelle slowly gained strength, she wondered ever more obsessively whether the man she'd known as Ernst Bauer had survived. Every day she waited eagerly for the mail. Surely someone would write to tell her what had happened to the prisoner whose identity she'd helped reveal. Why hadn't Stephen Yost or another MI agent contacted her? She phoned the Army hospital, asking to speak to staff members she'd known, but they'd all deployed elsewhere.

Because Isabelle couldn't concentrate for long, doctors advised rest for her damaged brain, and so she continued to spend several hours a day on the sleeping porch watching birds cavort outside the window. Leaves turned from green to gold to red and then fell to the ground. When it snowed in mid-November, Isabelle and her mother spread more seeds on the birdfeeder outside the dining room.

Chapter 9

In the last hours of 1944, Isabelle and Billy set a goal for their recovery. They promised each other that before July Fourth of 1945 they'd dance the jitterbug in a local club. They beat the deadline by a month. By June they were spending every weekend dancing, overcoming their inhibitions with illegal gin. Their limps didn't slow them down. The partying provided a temporary escape from wildly fluctuating emotions.

President Roosevelt had died in April, a heavy blow. In May, Isabelle and Billy had celebrated victory in Europe one day and wept the following day over newspaper photographs of emaciated prisoners and dead bodies in concentration camps. In July, they fretted that war in the Pacific would drag on forever. Then, when their country detonated atomic bombs over Hiroshima and Nagasaki, Isabelle and Billy stayed awake much of the night, unable to celebrate because of the horror unleashed by those weapons.

Billy was living on the family ranch and preparing to take over his father's job of raising and selling cattle. Each weekend he drove to Topeka, bunked with a friend at the Army Airfield, and spent his waking hours with Isabelle, leaving after dinner on Sunday. Her father referred to Billy as Isabelle's "heavy." She and Billy often drove into the Flint Hills and made slow, sweet love on the back seat of his parents' Buick Roadmaster, grateful for the big car.

One hot Saturday morning in August, they were sitting

at the breakfast table at the Graham's house when letters swished through the slot in the front door. Dr. Graham had left for the hospital, and Anne was shopping. Isabelle went to see what had arrived and noticed a small envelope with a "V" on the front—mail from a soldier overseas. In the upper left-hand corner was a name: Captain Stephen Yost. Guessing what was inside, she stood for a while passing the envelope like a hot coal from one hand to the other. When Billy came looking for her, they went into the living room and sat down on the couch. Isabelle read aloud.

July 31, 1945
Dear Isabelle,

> *I apologize that I couldn't write sooner to tell you that our mutual friend died from his wounds after we left Kansas. He was able to talk in his last days. I'm due for a furlough soon and can hitch a ride to the Topeka airfield. Please tell me how to reach you when I arrive.*

> *Sincerely,*
> *Captain Stephen Yost*

When she finished reading the letter, Isabelle looked up and saw Ernst Bauer again in the stall of the Buffalo Ridge barn. He has just revealed his true identity, and she demands that he flee with her on Joe. Again, Bauer refuses, but this time Isabelle threatens him with Billy's gun, and they escape to Daniel Jones' farm.

Imagining what might have been makes Isabelle weep. If she had threatened Bauer then, he'd be alive now. She knows that Yost's reference to Bauer being "able to talk" means that he—whatever his real name was—provided useful intelligence. Yost is clearly proud; Isabelle is wracked with shame.

She implores her brain to finally reveal what happened that afternoon. Who pulls the trigger of the gun? No matter how hard she tries, she can't remember. She imagines herself shooting the big sergeant to stop him from beating Bauer to death. Then she creates another scenario in which she gives Bauer the Colt .45, and he shoots Sergeant Schneider. But what about the second dead prisoner, Private Müller? Who shoots him? Nothing Isabelle can imagine rings true to her. Something is missing.

Coming back to herself, Isabelle told Billy she'd have no peace until she discovered what happened in the prison ward that day. "I'll have to investigate on my own," she said, "but I won't be too proud to request help when I need it."

That evening, after Billy left for the ranch, Isabelle answered Stephen Yost's letter and also wrote to Diane, who was due for another furlough. "I'm ready to unlock the past," Isabelle told her cousin. "Perhaps you can help."

Ten days later, and without notice, Diane appeared at the Grahams' front door. She hadn't yet been discharged from the Army but could now reveal where she'd lived and worked during most of the war. Impressed by her brilliance, the Army had loaned her to British intelligence in London. Most of the high-profile German POWs with potentially important scientific or technical knowledge were interrogated there. Diane reviewed transcripts, explained words and concepts to interrogators and suggested further questions. She worked as part of a team of experts in various academic disciplines.

She and Isabelle spent their first day together getting reacquainted. Isabelle had been only half a person when Diane visited before, but they quickly regained the intimacy they'd enjoyed as children. Isabelle read Agent Yost's letter to her cousin and described what had happened in the barn after the ride with Bauer.

"When he revealed that he was a Luftwaffe major, I should have forced him to leave with me. Military Intelligence Captain Yost could have spirited him away to safety. Instead, I returned him to the prison ward, a fatal error. My last memory from that day is sprinting back to the barn for the gun. I can see myself pulling it out from a saddlebag, but then what happened? An impenetrable darkness descends when I try to remember. Did I shoot the other two prisoners to save Bauer? Not knowing is making me crazy."

"Your psyche may be doing you a favor by not letting you remember."

"I *have to* learn if I killed those men."

The next morning, Diane arrived at the bungalow early and ordered Isabelle to follow her into the sunroom at the back of the house. It was hot, but shade from trees in the backyard kept that room fairly comfortable. Diane placed two chairs facing each other and gestured for Isabelle to sit across from her. After pulling out a pad and paper from her bag, Diane asked her cousin to describe their apartment in Vienna.

Isabelle fought the urge to leave the room. She hadn't talked about Vienna with anyone except superficially with her parents, but now she forced herself to describe the high ceilings, ornate moldings, and shiny wood floors of their apartment. Knowing her cousin would be interested, Isabelle also mentioned the flickering gold of gaslight outside her bedroom window.

"Electricity may be a blessing, but the world by gaslight can be magical," Diane said. "Now tell me about Otto Mauer."

Again, Isabelle wanted to bolt, but taking deep breaths, she managed to describe Otto as about the same height as herself and Diane. He had dark brown eyes and thick, curly, black hair and projected a physical and intellectual vitality that Isabelle and her parents had found irresistible.

"Did you love him?"

"I had a schoolgirl crush and also loved him like a brother."

"What in his teaching most influenced you?"

Isabelle thought for a minute and then explained that Otto used fairy tales to teach not only the German language, but also a philosophy of life. Evil existed powerfully in the world and must be resisted, as in the tales.

"I remember that he sometimes expressed optimism and pessimism in the same sentence. One time he said, 'German culture is about to turn lethal, but it won't last forever.' He believed that vengeance is a good antidote to evil. That's why he admired the 'The Juniper Tree.'"

"You mentioned that story to me after you returned."

"It was our favorite of the Grimms' tales. A little boy is murdered and cut into pieces by his stepmother, who cooks and feeds them to the boy's father. Marlinchen, the boy's sweet half-sister, gathers his bones, and weeping tears of blood, lays them in green grass under the juniper tree in their yard. Fire and mist rise from the tree, and from them, a wondrous bird emerges. It's the little boy, magically transformed. The bird kills the stepmother, making possible the final scene, which, thanks to Otto, I can recite in both German and English."

The bird threw the millstone on her head so that she was completely smashed. The father and Marlinchen heard this and came out. There were steam and flames and fire rising from the place, and when that was over, the little brother stood there, and he took his father and Marlinchen by the hand, and the three of them were so happy and went into the house and sat down at the table, and ate together.

"Otto considered the peaceful dinner table a universal symbol of harmony," Isabelle said.

Diane asked what the story had taught Isabelle.

"Avenging evil can restore harmony to your world."

Diane rose from her chair and went to the front hall to call Anne and William down from upstairs. Isabelle was surprised to learn that her father had stayed home. They came into the study and sat next to each other on a daybed along the wall. Anne turned on a floor fan in the corner of the room. It whirred softly in the background, the sound of summer in Kansas. Light filtering through leaves in the breezy back yard flickered on the wall. Diane first addressed Anne.

"Aunt Anne, what happened to Isabelle's tutor in Vienna?"

"Why do you want to know?"

"It haunts her still."

"I tried to block her from seeing the worst," Anne said, "but perhaps she witnessed more than we knew."

"What would she have witnessed?"

"A bloody nightmare."

Isabelle began to shake in her chair.

William continued the narrative. "An Austrian soldier shot Otto in a political uprising which grew into a short civil war. Otto came to me to extract the bullet. The police would have arrested him in any hospital. The bullet had lodged deeper than he—or we—thought, and something went wrong—perhaps he threw a clot during surgery. The memory of that night haunts Anne and me, as it does you, Isabelle. Otto stopped breathing, and we had to try to revive him before we'd completely closed the wound. There was a lot of blood. He cried out. You heard him and came running...."

Diane interrupted. "Let Isabelle tell what she remembers."

A cry and then uncontrolled keening. Anne saw that her daughter was about to fall from her chair and ran to hold her. Several minutes passed. Anne brought another chair from the dining room and sat next to Isabelle, holding her hand.

"The sound of something dying woke me up," Isabelle said. "I thought an animal had been hit by a car. It was a horrible sound. I ran to tell Mother and was sliding around the corner of the hall in my stocking feet when I saw her on the other side of a table in the living room. She cried tears of blood, like Marlinchen in 'The Juniper Tree.' There was something on the table, but I told myself that it couldn't be Otto because he told us he wasn't seriously injured. Mother was wiping blood from her face and hands with the towel we'd used earlier to dry dishes."

Anne interrupted. "I took you back to your room, and you seemed alright the next morning. We thought we'd prevented you from seeing the worst. We didn't want you to learn that Otto had died in our living room. We told you his father had come for him after the surgery, which was true. He came for Otto's body."

"I remember you saying that Otto had left on his own," Isabelle countered, "and when we didn't see him again, you claimed that he couldn't tutor me anymore because of his role in the uprising."

Close to weeping, Isabelle's father said, "I don't remember exactly what we said, but I recognize now that not revealing the whole truth was a terrible mistake.

Diane's questioning unleashed in Isabelle and her parents a flood of memories. After Diane left that day, Anne and

William revealed to Isabelle that they'd stayed up late in Vienna talking with Otto many nights after Isabelle went to bed. "Remember that he took the three of us to the theater?" Anne asked. "He introduced us to works we wouldn't have found on our own. We always paid, and you also came to every show. I remember especially a performance of a work by George Bernard Shaw translated by an Austrian playwright."

Isabelle told her parents about adventures with Otto she hadn't shared before, including racing on rented horses in the Prater and attending workers' rallies near his home. Then, late in the evening, Isabelle's father revealed for the first time that he and Anne had sometimes provided medical care in Vienna to Jews and other escapees from Hitler's Germany.

"You learned in school that Topeka was a stop on America's Underground Railroad, right?" William asked his daughter.

"Yes."

"And you know that your ancestors were involved in the Railroad?"

"Yes."

"When our minister heard that I'd received a fellowship to study in Vienna, he raised money from parishioners and asked Anne and me to deliver it to an Underground Railroad from Germany through Vienna. He had read about it somewhere. I taught Anne basic medical skills, and, in safe houses, we treated ill and injured escapees on their way to Italy and eventually Portugal, where—in those years—they could usually get passage on a freighter to the United States or Latin America."

Otto had somehow discovered what Isabelle's parents were doing, and, wounded, had sought their medical expertise for himself. Weeping, Isabelle told her mother and father that if they'd been truthful, they could have comforted each other. Instead, she'd faced sorrow and despair alone.

"I searched for Otto for many years after he disappeared," she told them. "When I didn't find him, I worried that he might be dead but forced myself to believe otherwise. I envied the little boy in 'The Juniper Tree' who became a bird to avenge his own death. Maybe I could do the same for Otto, I thought. Sometimes I even repeated to myself the bird's song in the story."

My mother who butchered me,
My father who ate me,
My sister, Marlinchen,
She gathered up my bones,
And tied them in a silken cloth,
To lay beneath the juniper tree,
Kiwitt, kiwitt, what a pretty bird I am!

The next morning, Diane asked Isabelle if she had so willingly agreed to interpret at Buffalo Ridge because it might provide the opportunity to avenge Otto's death.

"Maybe. I don't remember it being that specific, but it seemed evident that fate had somehow intervened."

The following day, the cousins spent the morning making lists of questions for head nurse Margaret McGrath, Stephen Yost, John Clevenger, and others Isabelle would question. Finally, Diane folded her notebook and put down her pen. "I've had enough," she said. "It's time to meet your Billy Greenwood."

Because William was a doctor, the Grahams were not subjected to gas rationing. In the family Buick, Isabelle and Diane drove southwest from Topeka through hills they'd explored as children, cooling off at favorite springs and wading in Lake Wabaunsee, where they'd ridden bareback into deep water and rejoiced in the power of a swimming horse.

When they reached Council Grove, Isabelle drove down Main Street, a segment of the old Santa Fe Trail, and stopped at a payphone. The Greenwood ranch was about ten miles away. Billy came in a truck to lead them over dirt roads that didn't exist on any map. Isabelle had met his parents over dinner in Topeka and enjoyed their good-humored intelligence, which Billy shared, but this was her first visit to the ranch. Three generations of Greenwoods had lived there. Stepping out of the car, she saw a large, two-story home which looked both very old and daringly new. It took Isabelle a few minutes to figure out that it was a remodeled Sears Roebuck catalogue home. In the early years of the century, many farmhouses in Kansas and other prairie states had been constructed from designs and components ordered from catalogues. Painted bright blue with white trim and with larger than usual first story windows and two new screened-in porches, the house looked like none Isabelle had ever seen. Beyond it were beds of roses and other cultivated flowers, and beyond them, a stream running through a pasture where Thoroughbred horses grazed. Cattle dotted the surrounding hills.

"Heaven," the cousins exclaimed. "Heaven!"

That afternoon and for the next two days, while Billy worked, Diane and Isabelle rode two of the horses in an ever-expanding radius around the ranch. Isabelle had gotten in shape dancing with Billy, taking long walks, and in recent weeks, riding Joe. The cousins recited names of prairie grasses—blue grama, big bluestem, sideoats grama—and behaving like children again, searched draws for potential hideouts like Wildland. They cantered often, and if they lost the trail, sometimes walked the horses to avoid prairie dog holes.

At night, after supper with Billy and his parents, the cousins stayed up late talking in the bunkhouse. Diane said she'd leave the Army soon and enroll in the school of medicine at the University of Kansas to study psychiatry. In London, she had befriended soldiers with battle fatigue and wanted to learn how to cure it. Isabelle said she couldn't predict what she would do next. Marry Billy? Work for a newspaper? Her future was on hold until she completed her investigation.

On the last afternoon of riding, Billy led the cousins to a high point on the ranch to watch a storm approach. The barometer had been falling, and they heard thunder in the distance. From the hilltop they watched roiling, cumulonimbus clouds draw ever closer. When a dark funnel suddenly formed and just as rapidly disappeared, Billy said it was time to go.

They rode hard and battened down hatches back at the ranch. The storm broke with howling winds, lightning, and hail, followed by sheets of cooling rain, which brought the horses up from their refuge by the creek. They ran like colts around the pasture. Finally—no bugs or heat. They were happy, and so were Diane and Isabelle.

Chapter 10

Military Intelligence officer Stephen Yost received Isabelle's letter and arrived in Topeka at the end of August. He called her and suggested they meet for lunch the next day at a café in the Jayhawk Hotel, where he was staying. Anne and William needed the car that day, so Isabelle walked the mile to the café. The temperature was in the 90s, and she arrived sweating and irritable. Watching through a window before entering, she saw Yost order a busy waiter to push a table into a corner where his conversation with Isabelle wouldn't be overheard. Isabelle had forgotten how commanding Yost could be. He wore stylish pants and a well-ironed white shirt. Isabelle wore a sleeveless yellow blouse and a wrinkled linen skirt, which she now tried to press with her hands. She entered the café, shook hands perfunctorily with Yost, and sat down at his corner table. They ordered sandwiches. No one spoke. Isabelle wanted him to go first.

"How are you?" Yost finally asked. She guessed he meant to give her an opportunity to describe her physical ordeal, but she wouldn't do that. Instead, she asked in what she hoped was an icy tone, "Why didn't you tell me earlier that Ernst Bauer had died?"

Yost nodded his head, a rueful recognition that this reunion wouldn't be easy.

"Crossed wires, I suppose. I went overseas soon after Major Meier died and thought my superiors would inform you of his death. Those were fraught times for all of us in Military Intelligence."

"Who's Major Meier?"

"That's the real name of Ernst Bauer. You didn't know? He was a Luftwaffe major named Johann Meier."

"In the barn that day he admitted to being a fighter pilot but never revealed his name."

Yost looked perplexed. He hadn't considered what Isabelle might not know.

"We have a lot to discuss," he said. "How should we proceed?"

Isabelle suggested that she begin by telling him what she remembered about her last day at the hospital. He could fill in gaps in her knowledge.

"Something had changed in Bauer that final morning," she said. "When he asked to go riding, I realized he wanted to talk to me alone and so I went for the necessary permissions. I assumed that the aide to MP Captain Freeland would inform you."

"I didn't return until later than I'd anticipated. No one told me that you'd taken Bauer—I mean Major Meier—riding."

"If they had, would you have stopped me?"

"No. Meier's information was worth the risk."

Isabelle recounted what Meier had told her in the barn. "After that, I insisted that the prison ward was too dangerous, and he should flee with me on my horse. He refused."

Yost assured her that she'd done the right thing. "Meier was a proud man and wanted to be removed by an officer with the power to grant his demands. But after leaving him at the ward you went back for him. What made you do that?"

"I suddenly realized that the other prisoners had to be hiding. Perhaps I had heard them subconsciously when I left Bauer behind."

Yost said that three days after the attack he'd taken Meier by plane to Walter Reed Hospital in Washington, D.C., a half-hour's drive from the secret interrogation center used by German-speaking American agents of Military Intelligence to interrogate high-profile POWs brought to this country. Meier had regained consciousness at Walter Reed. He remembered being jumped in the prison ward by Schneider. Meier said he'd resisted the bludgeoning, even grabbing the weapon and landing some blows of his own, but that didn't last long. Getting control of the studded board again, Schneider drove Meier into a wall and then down to the floor. Meier remembered nothing after that. He did not know that you returned to the ward to save him. The other prisoner, Private Müller, didn't participate in the attack on Meier but made no effort to stop it."

"I hope you told Meier that I came back to the prison ward."

"Yes. He correctly believed that you saved his life and wanted to thank you. With my help, he tried several times to reach you at the hospital in Topeka, but you didn't regain consciousness until after he'd died.

"For how long after the attack did he survive?"

"Seven days. He became fairly clear-minded and told us a lot in the middle of that week, but on the fifth day, he developed sepsis. I never got him to our interrogation center but questioned him at Walter Reed."

"The sepsis killed him?"

"That and damage to his brain, spleen, and liver."

Isabelle steeled herself against breaking down. *Meier didn't have to die. She and Stephen Yost were to blame for Meier's death and also for the death of Schneider and Müller.*

She didn't say that aloud but told Yost that she could not imagine a sequence of events that would end with her shooting both prisoners. "Perhaps I gave the gun to Meier before he blacked out, and he shot Schneider. Was the gun checked for fingerprints?"

"I was transferred to Europe shortly after Meier died and never saw the forensic expert's conclusions or the report provided by Clevenger to the Provost Marshall General."

Near tears, Isabelle held her head in her hands.

"I wouldn't have left Bauer/Meier dying in that room unless I was pursued by one of the attackers. Perhaps I shot Schneider, dropped the gun, and Müller picked it up and came after me. But then who shot him? I have more questions than answers."

Yost said that a nurse had seen Isabelle running across the hospital grounds from the prison ward, noticed that she was bleeding, and alerted MPs. They found Meier in the storage room near death. A physician came quickly and gave him emergency treatment. MPs carried him to the ICU, where a surgeon operated to ease pressure on his brain.

"So, we had similar injuries," Isabelle said.

"Yes, you were both hit with a nail-studded board. By the time I got to the prison ward, Meier had been removed. The other two men lay dead on the blood-splattered floor. I was allowed to stay in the room only a few minutes because MPs were protecting the crime scene.

"What did you see?"

"Schneider lay to the left of the door of the storage room. He had deep wounds in his back. I figured you or Meier had pried the weapon from his hands and beaten him with it. Schneider was shot twice, I think. Müller lay closer to the door. He'd also been shot."

"Do you know for sure that the gun I brought from the barn was used to shoot them?"

"I do not know that for sure, but it was probably in the final report. The storage room does have a window. Carpenters had been building new shelves in that room and we believe that they forgot to lock that window."

"I don't remember ever seeing a window in that ward when I walked or rode around the hospital grounds."

"Another shooter coming into the ward through that window seems unlikely. You had the gun and the motivation to use it. I assume you used the gun to save Meier, and I salute you for that. His information saved many Allied lives."

"Tell me about him."

"He'd received awards for his kills as a Luftwaffe fighter pilot. He was born and raised in the Währing district of Vienna, graduated from Gymnasium, entered the military, and was trained as an officer in the Austrian army. He opposed Hitler's invasion of Austria, but did not resist, unlike some of his fellow officers. After that, the Luftwaffe recruited Meier, and he rose quickly. At some point, Luftwaffe Commander Göring ordered Meier and a few other senior pilots to test the Me 262, a fighter jet known as the Schwalbe or Swallow. Meier said that Hitler never believed in the Schwalbe and instead directed dwindling resources to the jet-powered fighter bomber known as the Sturmvogel, the Stormbird.

"Meier told me that he'd never been a Nazi. Is that true?"

"As far as we can tell neither Meier nor any member of his family joined the Nazi Party or sympathized with Hitler. After their family doctor, a Jew, disappeared into a concentration camp in 1940, the Meiers became quiet but active opponents of Hitler and his party. When the major was shot down over North Africa and disappeared, his parents and sister hoped he had deserted. The family fled to northern Italy where a relative provided refuge. Meier's only demand was that we save his parents and sister, and we have done that.

"Where are they now?"

"I don't know and couldn't tell you if I did. Another intelligence branch took care of that. After Meier was shot down over North Africa and his name didn't appear on any prisoner lists, the high command of the Luftwaffe circulated his description to camps around the world and ordered POWs to watch for him. The bully Schneider must have known about that. It took him a while, but eventually he figured out that Bauer was Major Meier. Perhaps he guessed Meier revealed himself to you on the day you took him riding. It also took *us* a while to put Meier's disappearance together with information from Captain Freeland about the probable imposter at Buffalo Ridge."

"I never should have taken Meier back to the prison

ward," Isabelle said.

"He knew what he was doing. You accomplished something important. Without training, you identified an imposter and saved his life long enough for us to gather crucial information. I remember laughing when he told me that his relationship with you was 'an unusual alliance of interests that gave me the confidence to seek a new life elsewhere.' Of course, he fell in love with you. I wonder if Agent Clevenger included that in his report."

"I need to see that report," Isabelle said.

"Well, I've never read it and doubt it'll see the light of day. The Army succeeded in keeping the Buffalo Ridge attack from public knowledge and will resist any attempt to revisit it."

"You owe me the report," Isabelle insisted. "You and I are to blame for the deaths of three men. If I'd known that other POWs in the United States were actively looking for a potential imposter, I would have more vigorously insisted that you transfer the bullying sergeant. You'll remember that I asked you to do that when we first met, and if you'd granted my request, Meier would be alive now. He and the other prisoners are dead because of our failures."

Yost bristled. "Meier lived long enough to provide facts pertinent to the invasion. You can perhaps imagine the worrisome gaps in our intelligence in those months of preparation. Planners needed to know whether Hitler might suddenly produce a fleet of jet fighters that could overwhelm ours. Major Meier revealed that the Me 262 would be used in ever-greater numbers but never enough to challenge Allied air domination. He also told us where parts for the plane were manufactured, and we took out some of those under-ground factories. Meier wasn't the only person providing that information—hundreds of other pieces of intelligence had to be put together—but his contribution was critical. Al-lied commanders were pretty sure that we dominated the air by then, and Meier and others confirmed it. Your work and mine have received high commendations. I'm proud of it, and you should be too."

"When did MI first realize that Corporal Ernst Bauer was actually Major Johann Meier?"

"The missing Luftwaffe pilot had grown up in Währing, so when we heard that Bauer had also lived there, we thought he might be the one."

"And yet, even after I requested the removal of Sergeant Schneider from the prison ward, you left him in place?"

"It was the right thing to do."

"You and I are responsible for three unnecessary deaths. Please find Captain Clevenger and ask him to contact me. I have nothing more to say to you."

Chapter 11

Walking home that hot afternoon, Isabelle regretted not playing on Yost's sympathies by describing her difficult recovery. Instead, she had put him on the defensive by accusing him of causing three deaths, and now she feared he might not help her find the investigator, Captain Clevenger. She was passing a Buick dealership on Jackson and 6th Street when it hit her that Stephen Yost's sins were minor compared to her own. He'd made a bad decision in not removing Sergeant Schneider from the ward, but she'd most likely shot two men to death. If Bauer/Meier's revelations saved the lives of Allied soldiers, did that mitigate Yost's and her sins? Isabelle pondered that as she turned onto 3rd Street and headed west toward home. A gust of wind rustled a canopy of leaves above her, bringing to mind "The Juniper Tree."

The juniper began to stir and the branches kept opening out and joining together again... And with this, a kind of mist was coming out of the tree, and in the middle of the mist it burned like fire, and out of the fire flew a most beautiful bird who sang so wonderfully and soared high up into the air...

Isabelle wondered why that part of the tale in particular came back to her as she weighed her own guilt. The bird that flew from the tree was an instrument of vengeance. Had she taken Billy's gun into the prison ward to avenge her tutor's death? If so, she'd committed pre-meditated murder, a serious criminal and moral offense. Or did she grab the gun not to avenge Otto but to save Meier's life, which was morally defensible?

If I hadn't taken the pistol, Meier wouldn't have lived seven more days and mitigated his own sins by helping us win the war, Isabelle thought.

Meier had called himself *ein Experte* which meant he'd killed many Allied pilots. He was the enemy, but Isabelle couldn't forget him saying that he was glad an Allied pilot had shot him down. Though Meier had suffered months of pain and amnesia after his plane fell from the sky, he was grateful to have been forcibly removed from battle. He preferred suffering to killing on behalf of Adolf Hitler.

Back home in the Grahams' living room, Isabelle lay on the couch in the breeze of a table fan. After a few minutes, still agitated by her encounter with Yost, she jumped up and dialed the number for Buffalo Ridge Hospital. An operator told her that chief nurse Margaret McGrath had long ago been transferred to the Army Hospital in Nashville. The operator gave Isabelle that number, and surprisingly, after a few rings, McGrath answered. Isabelle explained that she had begun her own investigation of the Buffalo Ridge killings. After a long silence, McGrath said she'd been transferred to Nashville two weeks after the *altercation.*

"That's what the hospital called it," McGrath said with disdain.

"Why were you transferred?"

"It could have been routine. Isabelle, I don't have time to talk. What do you want?"

"Information. I won't have peace of mind until I learn what happened in the prison ward. Did Private Schmitt, the opera singer, reveal anything before he left the hospital?"

"Schmitt knew nothing about the attack. I heard that the two dead prisoners were shot to death. Did you shoot them?"

"That's the mystery I'm trying to solve. Where were the MPs? They must have heard the attack in the guard house."

"They were escorting a Red Cross volunteer to another building. They returned to the ward just after you fled."

McGrath surprised Isabelle then.

"I'd heard rumors that Nazis in prison camps in this country were threatening and sometimes even attacking fellow prisoners suspected of turning stool pigeon and figured it could also happen at an Army hospital. I don't know German military law, but it makes sense that Schneider and Müller would consider it their duty to prevent Bauer from revealing military secrets to the enemy. How could they do that without killing him? In similar circumstances, our own soldiers might have done the same."

Someone called to McGrath then—an emergency, she said, and hung up the phone.

Isabelle sat down at the desk in the living room to make notes about her first day of detection.

Chapter 12

A few days later, Captain John Clevenger called Isabelle at home. Yost had found him still serving in the Criminal Investigation Division of the Army's Seventh Services Headquarters in Omaha. Clevenger agreed to talk to Isabelle, and the next day, she drove north to Auburn, Nebraska, a town halfway between Omaha and Topeka. Clevenger had suggested meeting on the grounds of the Auburn County Courthouse, a 19th–century limestone beauty. She found him sitting at a picnic table, reading in the shade of old elm and oak trees. He rose, smiling, as she approached.

"I'm glad to see that you've not only survived, but apparently thrived," he said.

He told her he'd visited her in Stormont Hospital nearly every day during the time he was in Topeka, but she'd never regained consciousness.

"Are you feeling as good as you look?"

"More or less," she replied.

She asked Clevenger about his background and learned that he had grown up on Lake Michigan in Chicago and attended high school there. He'd graduated from Yale College in Connecticut three years before Isabelle graduated from Wellesley. He surprised her by asking about her parents and also about Jake Newman and Billy Greenwood. He'd found them deeply distressed when he was in Topeka and hoped they'd recovered. His concern for them impressed Isabelle.

On the telephone, she had explained her need to investigate, and now she asked her most important question.

"Did I kill Schneider and Müller with Billy Greenwood's gun?"

"The evidence was inconclusive," Clevenger said.

Isabelle asked if he'd considered potential scenarios.

"Of course, but neither I nor the forensic expert could substantiate them. Sergeant Schneider and Private Müller were each shot twice. Only your prints on the pistol were definitively decipherable, but there were faint traces of other prints as well. You and Major Meier were severely beaten by the same weapon. That's why your wounds were similar. From what I saw in that room, I could envision several scenarios, but please don't assume any is correct. Maybe you came into the storage room, found Schneider in the act of battering Meier, and somehow got ahold of the weapon. That would explain the wounds on Sergeant Schneider's head and back. Then Schneider got back the weapon, and you shot him to save Meier and yourself. The coroner reported that Schneider died from a bullet that pierced his aorta. In this imagined scenario, Müller then comes for you with his own nail-studded weapon, and you shoot him too."

"Do you know how long I was in the prison ward?"

"We estimated 15 or 20 minutes at the most. A nurse saw you go in and someone else saw you run, bleeding, toward the barn. What do you remember?"

"Nothing from the time I got the gun in the barn. According to the doctors, I won't recover the memory. They believe it's a result of brain damage and not psychological trauma. Did you inform the Topeka police about the killings?"

"The International Red Cross, Swiss Government, and U.S. Army came to an agreement about how to handle that. I don't know exactly what they did. I haven't read the law myself but have heard that it's legal under German military law in some circumstances to kill a fellow prisoner believed to have turned stool pigeon. Perhaps the families of Schneider and Müller were told their loved ones died heroically. I wouldn't know about that, but they were informed about the deaths.

Isabelle was relieved. She had suffered the psychic cost of a loved one disappearing without a trace.

She said, "I strongly believe that Meier and the others died because of avoidable mistakes."

"What mistakes?"

"First, Captain Yost denied my request to remove Schneider from the prison ward. Second, MPs left the ward unguarded. And third, I failed to force Meier to flee. If I'd used Billy Greenwood's pistol to make him leave the barn with me, the three prisoners would still be alive."

Clevenger didn't argue with that. Instead, he said simply that he understood and sympathized with Isabelle's desire to learn the truth. She asked if she could have a copy of his report to the Provost Marshall General, but he hadn't been allowed to keep one. He had, however, kept notes.

"I'll go through them to see if I've forgotten something that might help your quest. In that case, you'll hear from me."

They chatted for a while longer in the shade of the sheltering trees. Clevenger mentioned that her parents had referred to a loss in Vienna that had blighted their time there. "They provided no details, but I wondered if there could be a connection between that loss and your decision to take a gun to the prison ward."

"I wonder the same thing," Isabelle said.

Afterward, they walked together to their cars and drove off in different directions. Isabelle figured she'd never see him again.

Chapter 13

A week later, Isabelle received a letter from Captain Clevenger. Though he'd found nothing in his notes worth reporting, he gave her the name and phone number of Dr. Lattimore, the forensic expert. Isabelle called him but learned nothing new. "Not all murders are solved," he said. "The available evidence in this case did not permit definitive conclusions about who had killed whom."

In late September, when the days had cooled and leaves were just beginning to turn, Jake Newman came to Topeka from New York to visit his parents. Walking with Isabelle in Gage Park, he revealed that he'd fallen in love with an actress in New York, and Isabelle told him about her deep affection for Billy. She also shared what she'd learned so far in her investigation. Jake remembered being interrogated by Clevenger and also short conversations with MI Captain Yost.

"Hunting dogs, the two of them. Always sniffing for information. Good at it. Did Bauer give up anything useful?"

"Yes. He was actually a Luftwaffe Major, and his real name was Johann Meier. Stephen Yost considers our work a great success. I see mostly our mistakes."

Jake thought for a while and then pronounced his own verdict. "Yost came to Buffalo Ridge because he'd decided—based on what you were learning about Bauer..."

"Meier."

"Sorry. Yost had decided, based on what you'd learned,

that Meier was about to give up important information. It meant that you and Meier might both be in danger, but Yost left you both in place. Yes, it indicates some disregard for your life, but it also shows respect for what you'd accomplished so far and confidence in what you'd do next. He judged you quickly, but correctly, and he had faith that you could handle whatever happened. Perhaps, as you believe, Yost and you made flawed decisions, but they're defensible. Nobody I know from my experience in combat believes that he did everything right. Most of us soldiers—and you're one of us now—have punishing regrets. I've figured out how to live with mine, and in time you will do the same. I join Yost in saluting the difficult decisions you made at Buffalo Ridge."

In early October, Isabelle and Billy drove northwest from Topeka to the big prison camp at Concordia, where they asked to speak with the opera singer, Private Schmitt. A guard at the gate bewailed Schmitt's recent departure. He'd given concerts and was popular at the camp but had gone east for eventual repatriation.

On the way home, Isabelle admitted to Billy that she remained unhealthily fixated on learning if she'd killed the two prisoners. "I imagine myself walking into the storage room and firing away at Schneider and Müller. Or maybe I *beat* Schneider almost to death. Am I capable of pounding nails into a man's back? It seems important to know that."

Billy said he and members of his platoon had sometimes asked themselves similar questions after combat. "I remember little about the men I killed or the situations surrounding those deaths. I assume they were justified, but perhaps I'm wrong. I did what I had to do to protect my men and to survive myself, and so did you."

A few days later, on an October morning that shimmered in golden light, Isabelle's mother dropped her off at Daniel Jones's farm. He was in the barn, and Isabelle invited him to ride with her to Buffalo Ridge. She had seen workers digging the foundation of a new veterans' hospital in Topeka and wanted to visit Buffalo Ridge before it was completely torn down. On their horses, she and Daniel crossed the old limestone bridge and trotted up the same path she'd taken two years before, when she first rode Joe to the hospital. By chance, they arrived at the periphery fence close to the place where Joe had jumped after the attack. Across the hospital grounds were the medical wards where she'd served—some still in use, others in the process of demolition. They continued around the periphery fence, Daniel leading the way, and when they came up behind the prison ward, Isabelle noticed the large, low-down window that Stephen Yost had mentioned—the one left unlocked by carpenters. The window was closed but not barred. Through the fence and the razor wire that surrounded the ward, Isabelle saw boxes, shelves, mops, a broom.

She stopped Joe.

"I never noticed that window when I worked here," she said.

"This is where I watched you shoot the prisoners," Daniel responded.

Speechless, Isabelle stared at him.

"I told you before, I sometimes rode to Buffalo Ridge to check on Joe because I worried that prisoners would mistreat him. I was on Amber just outside the fence on the day you were injured. I saw you run very fast across the grounds toward the building surrounded by razor wire, which I figured must be the prison ward. I followed the fence to where we are now and watched through that window as you entered the room."

"What did you see?"

"Are you sure you want to know?

"Yes."

"A huge guy had cornered another man and was slamming him with a board. Suddenly you jumped on the attacker's back. It sounds crazy—you're small compared to that brute—but you got hold of his weapon and used it on him. I slid off Amber and climbed over the fence, cutting my hands and arms on the barbed wire and then again on the razor wire around the ward."

Pushing up his sleeves to show scars, he continued. "I saw the big man throw you off. He grabbed the board, which was studded with nails, and beat you. The window was unlocked, and I was about to enter the room when you pulled a pistol from your pocket and shot him twice. He fell to the floor. Shock paralyzed me. Then the other prisoner, who before had stayed back, came at you full force with another board. You shot him once before the gun slipped from your bloody hand. Downed but not dead, he grabbed the gun. You kicked him hard, and he dropped it. You picked it up and shot him a second time, but he kept crawling along the ground, grabbing at your feet. I came through the window just as you dropped the gun, turned, and fled the room. The hospital emergency sirens blew, and I got out of there as fast as I could. I suspect the second attacker died as I was fleeing. I didn't know where you'd gone, or I'd have followed you. Thank God Billy Greenwood chased you and saved your life. Since then, I've lived in fear that someone saw me leaving the ward and I'd be charged with the killings and have to testify against you to save myself. That prospect sickened me. I kept hoping you'd talk to me—at least say *something* about that day—but you never did."

At first Isabelle couldn't speak. She was shocked and angry with Daniel but also deeply sorrowful. One more life—his—damaged by her mistakes.

Finally, she explained that what Daniel had witnessed was wiped from her brain by the beating she took. "I didn't know for sure until now that I'd shot the two men."

They didn't speak as they rode back to the farm. Isabelle was reeling from his revelation, furious that he'd been silent for so long.

At the farm they unsaddled their horses and released them in the pasture. After that, they stood by the gate talking for a long time. Isabelle shared her guilt and shame and explained what she'd learned in her investigation. Daniel apologized for not telling her sooner what he'd witnessed. He'd gone into shock, he claimed. Grieving, Isabelle left the farm late that afternoon. Back home, she recounted Daniel's story to her parents. Her father called their minister, and the following Sunday afternoon, Isabelle told him what she'd learned. Over the next days, he listened sympathetically as she confronted the fact that she had shot two men to death.

Gradually Isabelle's anger at Daniel Jones faded. She understood that his judgment had for a time been destroyed by what he witnessed.

Learning the truth brought Isabelle little solace. She remained convinced that errors of judgment—hers and Stephen Yost's—had led to the deaths of the three prisoners. She also questioned the morality of revealing information about Major Meier to MP Captain Freeland. She'd been hired by Buffalo Ridge as an interpreter, not a spy.

But after some months Isabelle no longer felt crushed by shame. "I didn't shoot Schneider and Müller to avenge my tutor," she told her parents one night at supper. "I shot them to save the man I knew as Ernst Bauer and also to save myself. My tutor, our beloved Otto, played a role in what I did. The tales of vengeance he taught dramatized the avoidance of victimhood. I learned to recognize evil and refuse to be its victim. Otto made it obligatory for me to kill in order to save Major Meier and myself."

APRIL 1946

On this day, her last in Topeka for a long while, Isabelle dismounts from her horse and steps carefully to avoid shards of glass and wire as she says goodbye to the hospital at Buffalo Ridge. The periphery fence, the gate, and many buildings, including the barn, are gone. Shoots of bluestem and switchgrass push up across the grounds, signs of new life. Wind whips her, each gust carrying phantom voices and the music of Jake's piano. In the west, a fiery sun disappears below the horizon.

Six months have passed since Daniel Jones revealed the full story of the Buffalo Ridge killings. Isabelle has spent that time fitting together her own and others' memories like bones from an exhumation.

In last light, she will ride Joe back to the farm to tell Daniel Jones goodbye before returning home for dinner with her parents. Together at their table, the final scene of "The Juniper Tree" will come to her mind. Billy will arrive later, and he and Isabelle will weep when he leaves. Late in the evening, she'll place the final items of clothing in a new suitcase and, the next morning, fly from the Topeka Army Airfield to Nuremberg, Germany, to interpret for Captain John Clevenger, who is now investigating German war crimes.

Does she seek penance? Maybe, but what counts is the work ahead, which she recognizes is more important than her feelings of regret.

Billy says he'll wait for her.

She's made him no promises.

Afterword

Because I had long wanted to write a novel and needed inspiration, I experienced as a gift the sudden apparition before me one day of a woman on horseback staring at a man behind a barred window. I sensed they were in Kansas, where I grew up, and after some historical research, decided to feature them as characters in a novella. At first, I thought the woman on horseback might be an agent of Military Intelligence, but instead she became an interpreter driven by events beyond her control to spy on a wounded prisoner of war at an Army hospital in Kansas. Remembering that my grandfather had studied surgery in Vienna in the early part of the last century, I decided that Isabelle would be the daughter of a physician who learned German in that city, where she would witness bloody violence during a civil war.

To me, the Kansas prairie is wondrous and the words "Buffalo Ridge" evocative, hence the placement and name of my fictional U.S. Army hospital where wounded American soldiers and POWs are given the best medical treatment available at the time. Though Buffalo Ridge was partly inspired by Francis A. Winter General U.S. Army Hospital, which was near my home in Topeka, the characters and bloody events in this novella are entirely a product of my imagination. I learned in my research that suspected stool pigeons in POW camps around the United States had been threatened and even killed by fellow prisoners, but as far as I know, no such violence occurred at Winter General, which treated almost 1,000 prisoners of war between 1943 and 1946.

As a small child, I attended the First Presbyterian Church of Topeka with my parents. Later, I joined a youth group at a Congregational Church closer to home. The leader of that group vehemently opposed racial segregation and spoke often of the physical and moral injuries of war. He once invited a member of the U.S. armed services—I forget which branch—to our group to describe how he'd survived torture after being taken prisoner during the Korean war.

"The Juniper Tree," my favorite of the Grimms' tales, repeatedly came to mind as I wrote *Last Light,* eventually becoming an accompaniment to the story. Stefan Zweig is a character because I admire his fiction and especially his memoir, *The World of Yesterday.* He realized early that a genocidal war was coming.

I covered armed conflicts around the world as a reporter and have long wondered if I would be capable of killing someone to save my own or another person's life. My father kept guns for hunting in our Topeka home and taught my older sister, Marcia, and me to shoot when we were young. She received a .22 rifle and a horse for Christmas when she was 13 years old. No one in our family ever shot another person, and I hope that I'm never faced with a decision like Isabelle's at Buffalo Ridge.

ACKNOWLEDGEMENTS

I am deeply grateful to my agent, Amy Rennert, who vigorously championed this novella. Among her many talents she recently played on two tennis teams that won national championships, serving as captain of one and co-captain of the other.

Kudos and many thanks to editor/publisher Thea Rademacher, lawyer, author, owner of Flint Hills Publishing. She taught me a lot about publishing as we worked on *Last Light*, and her kindness, clear-thinking, and organizational skills made the process enjoyable

For our cover, the much-lauded photographer Terry Evans generously gave us permission to use part of one of her most striking prairie pictures. I am grateful to Terry for her generosity and friendship over many years. The whole photograph can be found in this collection:

www.terryevansphotography.com/farm

I thank my husband, Charles Farnsworth, our son Sam, and daughter Jenny, for their encouragement during many months of working on *Last Light*. Thanks also to their spouses, Charlotte and Chris, and our six grandchildren, who provide a joyful distraction from work.

Marion Abott, John Balaban, Douglas Foster, Michael Mosettig, Linda Spalding, and Ayelet Waldman read early drafts and provided positive praise. Many thanks to them. The following friends and colleagues also read and critiqued drafts: Tom Averill, Eleanor Bertino, Deborah Gee, Jeffrey Goudie, Kimberly Gregg, Brenda Hillman, Adam Hochschild, Arlie Russell Hochschild, Dr. Judith Kellman,

Mary Kay Mathiesen, Dr. H.C. Palmer, Eve Pell, Margaret Rowland, Dr. Charles Spezzano, Eric Stover, Rob Weiss, and Dorothy Witt. I thank you all.

At the Kansas Historical Society in Topeka, Bobbie Athon, Teresa Coble, Sarah Garten, and Sara Keckeisen located valuable information for me about the treatment of injured U.S. soldiers and POWs in WW II Kansas. For example, I learned from a November 21, 1943, *Topeka Daily Capital* article about the unloading of seriously injured American soldiers on litters through the windows of a train. Most helpful was a microfilm from the National Archives of the United States that contained weekly reports written for the Provost Marshall General of the United States on the number of prisoners at Kansas POW camps and U.S. Army military hospitals. I am grateful to the historical society and all who helped me there.

Air Force Col. (Ret.) Steven M. Kleinman wrote a superb thesis about MIS-Y, the branch of Military Intelligence responsible for conducting strategic interrogations of German and Japanese military officers and technical specialists at a secret facility near Washington, DC. The thesis is available at: apps.dtic.mil/dtic.mil/sti/citations/ADA447589.

I'm grateful for Steven Kleinman's willingness to answer my many questions. He is the recipient of Central Intelligence Agency and Defense Intelligence Agency elite human intelligence collector awards.

Dr. Virgil Dean, a historian of Kansas, read an early draft and gave me good advice about everything from John Brown to summer gardening in his state. He also referred me to Dr. Mark Hull, a professor at the Fort Leavenworth U.S.

Army Command and General Staff College, who wrote a fine piece in the journal, *Military Review*, about military law and vigilante justice in POW camps during World War II. I thank Virgil Dean for graciously sharing his knowledge of Kansas and Mark Hull for deepening my knowledge and understanding. I also thank Wendy Bevitt of Buried Past Consulting in Overbrook, Kansas, for researching on my behalf contemporaneous African American newspapers for information about racial segregation and the Double V campaign in Kansas during World War II. Ben Major, Administrator at the WW2 US Medical Research Centre, kindly answered my questions about segregation of U.S. Army Hospitals during that time.

Lynn Adler sought copyright clearances, a tough job. Many thanks to her.

Karina Epperlein translated *The Juniper Tree* and other works quoted in *Last Light*, consulting various sources published in German over the decades and now in the public domain. I observed her repeatedly ponder words in English to adequately express the magic of, among others, the Brothers Grimm. I am deeply grateful for her poetic sensibility and close attention to detail. Karina came to San Francisco from Germany in her late twenties to perform with an American theater company. Since then, she has created original theater pieces, made documentary films, and teaches the Art of T'ai Chi Ch'uan. She writes a regular blog spot: karinalandriver.blogspot.com.

FOR FUTHER READING

Last Light is a novella based mostly on my imagination, which was encouraged and deepened by the following sources, among others:

From the Kansas State Historical Society, Topeka, Kansas:

Articles from *The Topeka State Journal* and *The Topeka Daily Capital;The Sunflower* (a publication of Topeka's Winter General U.S. Army Hospital during the war); *Annual Report, 1944*, Winter General Hospital; "Stalag Sunflower, German Prisoners of War in Kansas," by Patrick O'Brien, Thomas D. Isern, and R. Daniel Lunley, *Kansas History*. Vol. 7 #3, Autumn 1984; and, most importantly for me, a microfilm from the National Archives of the United States (MS960.01), United States Provost Marshal General's Bureau, POW Ops Division, POW Records, 1942-'46, Reel # 66,538, Office of the Provost Marshal General, Weekly Reports on Prisoner of War Tabulations.

The following books and articles were especially helpful:

Adams, Meredith Lentz, *Murder and Martial Justice: Spying and Retribution in WW II America*, Kent State University Press, 2011.

Delmont, Matthew F., *The Epic Story of African Americans Fighting WW II at Home and Abroad*, Viking, 2022.

Hull, Mark M. "Option 17: Law and Vigilante Justice in Prisoner of War Camps During WW II," *Military Review,* January-February 2020.

Lamb, David, Prisoners of Silence, *Los Angeles Times*, November 30, 1990.

Morehouse, Maggi M., *Fighting in the Jim Crow Army, Black Men and Women Remember WW II*, Roman and Littlefield, 2000.

Prochnik, George, *The Impossible Exile: Stefan Zweig at the End of the World*, Other Press, 2023.

Rolf, David, *The Bloody Road to Tunis*, Greenhill Books and Stackpole Books, 2001.

Steinhoff, Johannes, Messerschmitts *Over Sicily, Diary of a Luftwaffe Fighter Commander*, Stackpole Military History Series, 2004.

Zweig, Stefan, *The World of Yesterday*, Translated by Anthea Bell, U. of Nebraska Press, 2013.

On-line versions of some works in German mentioned in the novella can be found here:

The Brothers Grimm, *Grimms' Fairy Tales: Children's and Household Tales*, www.grimmstories.com/en/grimm_ fairy-tales/index

The Brothers Grimm, *Kinder und hausmärchen: gesammelt durch die Brüder Grimm, Volumes 1-2,* books.google.com/books?id=y9tLAAAAI-AAJ&pg=PA232&hl=en#v=onepage&q&f=false

Rainer Maria Rilke's *Herbsttag (Autumn Day):* de.wikipedia.org/wiki/Herbsttag

Ihre Suchergebnisse, *Aphorsmen*, www.aphorismen.de/such e?f_thema=Liebe&f_autor=1167_Joseph+von+Eichendorff

Zweig, Stefan, *Angst: Internet Archive,* archive.org/details/angst00zwei

ABOUT THE AUTHOR

Elizabeth Farnsworth, documentary filmmaker and former chief correspondent of the PBS *NewsHour*, has written for publications ranging from *The Nation Magazine* to *Foreign Policy.*

Her memoir, *A Train Through Time: A Life, Real and Imagined,* was published by Counterpoint Press in 2017.

Farnsworth's documentary, *The Judge and the General,* co-produced with Patricio Lanfranco, premiered at the 2008 San Francisco Film Festival and aired on POV (PBS) and other networks around the world. As a print reporter and for television, she has covered crises in Iraq, Cambodia, Vietnam, Botswana, Chile, Peru, Haiti, Iraq, Iran, and Israel, among other countries.

Farnsworth grew up in Topeka, Kansas, where her ancestors were pioneers. She graduated magna cum laude from Middlebury College and earned an M.A. in Latin American History from Stanford University. She received an honorary doctorate degree from Washburn University (2021) and Colby College (2002). She has received three national Emmy nominations and the Alfred I. DuPont-Columbia Award, often considered the broadcast equivalent of the Pulitzer Prize, which is also administered by Columbia University.

Farnsworth serves on the advisory board of the Human Rights Center, UC Berkeley School of Law, and the advisory committee of the World Affairs Council of Northern California. She lives in Berkeley, California, with her husband, retired attorney Charles E. Farnsworth. They have three children and six grandchildren.

www.elizabeth-farnsworth.com

Made in the USA
Monee, IL
29 March 2024

55354863R00111